Copyright © 2020 by Peter Ashworth.

All of the characters in this book are fictitious and any resemblance to any actual persons living or dead is purely coincidental.

All rights reserved. This book or any portion thereof may not be reproduced or used in any manner whatsoever without the express written permission of the publisher except for the use of brief quotations in a book review.

Printed in the United States of America

First Printing, 2020

ISBN 9798646 109591.

Family, as always.

1.

I think we were all probably going to die today. We were parked in the yard of an abandoned cotton mill, abandoned long before the fighting started, when all of the work went overseas. Ironically, the ancestors of the people we were now fighting had come over to work in the cotton mills doing jobs that the English didn't want. I had six vehicles and 14 troops under my command. Sounds impressive but I was just a Sergeant vehicle specialist who had been attached to the mortar platoon to manage their motors.

We had been fighting our way across country for four days now; CW2-the second English Civil War, had erupted from almost nowhere, but we should have seen the warning signs with loads of militants coming back from overseas and seeming to have an endless supply of AK47's. Some people thought that it was all being stirred up by the Russians, but they were the same people who thought the Russians were responsible when Liverpool lost at home on the weekend- basically numptys!

The entire platoon command staff had been killed along with about a dozen of the troopers, that left me as the senior rank, and I was absolutely crapping myself. Trouble was the guys were looking to me for leadership and really, they were looking in the wrong place.

Our objective was a large fortified police station about a mile away, we had lost all comms days ago and as far as we could tell on the maps this was the nearest place we could hide until someone got organised and got us some help.

I had two land rovers and four trucks, packed to the roof with ammo and kit but we were about a mile from the nick and had to cross a park which was dark and seemingly empty.

There was a housing estate going up the hill on the right, the park in front of us and a river on the left, if we drove straight out into the park we would be wide open to fire coming from the estate which was occupied by the enemy. It was very quiet, about 2 o'clock in the morning and pitch black but that did not mean that there were not hordes of militants out there crouching behind their machine guns waiting to wipe us out.

'Fuck this' I thought, I have lost too many people to piss about. I called the guys into a group and said,

'Right, this is what we are going to do. I want half a dozen bombs dropping on that estate to keep them busy then we will make a dash for it across the park and we are not stopping for anyone.'

'Can't be done' said Tommo, he was a long serving mortar platoon Corporal and very experienced. 'We cannot fire on a civilian population, it's wrong on so many levels.'

'Do you want to live through this?' I said, 'because I do and these guys do, they have shot the shit out of us for four days and I am not risking a massacre down in that park.'

There was some murmuring from the other guys but basically, I had had enough.

'Corporal Thompson, plot me a track of six anti-personnel bombs across that estate,' he looked at me; I think he was trying to judge if I was serious.

I flicked the safety catch off my rifle and pointed it at his head,

'That is an order Corporal and we are in wartime conditions'

Everything went very quiet.

He must have seen the wild look in my eyes because he immediately gave some commands to his team.

They lifted a 'tube' off the land-rover and set it up. Tommo did some twiddling of the sights on the side and looked at me, I waved my hand in a circle which is the 'start engine's' command and heard the heavy diesel engines on the trucks firing up. I looked at Tommo and nodded, he said something to the team, and they dropped a bomb down the tube, it shot off with a roar and Tommo adjusted the sights and the process was repeated. Shit I thought, these guys were fast.

They had six bombs in the air and the tube back in the Landy before the first one hit. The effect was stunning, we were already moving out onto the street leading to the park, I was leaning out of the roof hatch and had a clear view. The bombs landed in a line across the estate, some on the streets and some directly through the rooves of the houses; the chaos must have been amazing.

We were at full speed now flying across the park heading for the small gate at the other end, I saw a muzzle flash as a weapon was fired at us from the darkness and fired a full magazine in return, as did the trooper in the rear Landy. We had loads of ammunition so this was not as reckless as you might think.

I changed mags and watched as the houses we had hit caught fire, people were visible in the flames running around, I was so brutalised by this stage in the operation that I just hoped they would be so distracted that we would be able to make it safely to our destination.

We drove straight through the small park gate, up the hill and down the other side coming up on the police station in front of us, our radio operator had been able to contact a security guard on his short-wave set and they were expecting us. It was a massive concrete building which had been designed with the riots of the early 80's in mind and that was paying off now, the metal shutters were down over the windows and as we approached the huge steel roller door on the vehicle bay chugged upwards and we drove into the massive underground garage.

There was a middle-aged security guy who was the only member of staff left in the building. He was very glad to see us and seemed to be under the impression that we had come to rescue him. Oh dear.

There were a few civvy cars and a minibus parked at the far end and a couple of Land Rovers near the lift. I marshalled our vehicles so we could unload into the lift and sent the guys back with an empty truck which they parked across the entrance, inside the roller door; it would not stop anyone who managed to open the door, but it would certainly slow them down.

The security guard was driving his car back towards the door, I waved him to a halt.

'I need to get going boss, I haven't seen my family for two days, I need to make sure that they are all right now that you are here to protect the women.'

What could I say, he was a brave guy and wanted to get back to his family? What women?

'If they ask you any questions tell them to stay away from this building or we will fuck them right up, ok?'

'Yes boss.'

We moved the truck and let him out, I watched him drive away and silently wished him luck. He would probably have been safer staying here with us, but his family had to come first, brave guy. Then we put the truck back in place.

The roller door was the problem, that was the point of entry for any enemy action. I had blocked it with the truck, but we needed to think about this.

I went up the stairs to the roof which was 5 floors up. It had been designed with a chest high wall around the edges with firing slits in, a little like an old-time crusader fort. It also leaned outwards slightly at the top which I was hoping was design feature rather than a problem with the foundations!

Tommo was supervising the unloading from the lift and was placing the mortar tubes to cover the main approaches which were on three sides as we still had the river on one side, it was fairly fast flowing and looked very polluted so I was hoping that the militants did not have their own version of the SBS but even if they swam the river there was just a solid wall on that side. The building was only overlooked by the clock tower of the gothic style town hall. I didn't think we would be in much trouble from there.

I went to have a look around the rest of the building and found a bunch of women and children in the gym area. These were military families heading back to a base in the Midlands who had been forced to stop here by the enemy action. There were 11 women and 31 children, the women were keeping them busy in the gym and the social centre which were deep inside the building, one of the women, Lisa, who was in charge, was very glad to see us.

She told me that there was plenty of food as the building had being designed to withstand a siege and had its own stock of food, water, medical supplies, fuel oil and generators. So far, they had been in the building for 5 days and whilst the militants had not attacked them, they were very frightened as to what might happen if they did. I reassured them as best I could that we would fight to the death to protect them. I sorted out some food and sleeping accommodation for the troopers and went back up to the roof.

The view from the roof was pretty good we could see probably six or seven hundred meters in each direction. Tommo had set up most of the tubes facing the estate with just one pointing down to the car park by the Town Hall. The troops were busy stacking ammunition and other weapons by the mortars. We each had our own personal weapons, SA80 rifles, but we also had sniper rifles, a couple of GPMG's (machine guns known as 'Gympys') and plenty of grenades, I was happy with what he was doing so I left him to it.

I noticed some large plastic containers on the roof, which looked a bit like those you see with life rafts in when you go on a booze cruise? I went over to one and saw that it had 'Escape System' stenciled on the top, it was sealed with cable ties, but I broke out my trusty Leatherman and sliced them off. Inside was a large flat metal bar attached to a massive coil of rope. In the lid were several pairs of leather gloves with extra layers on the palms, I had seen these before and used them a couple of times, these were 'fast roping' gloves.

So, the 'escape system' was a big rope and some leather gloves, don't fancy that I thought and reclosed the lid.

I expected that the militants would attack us as soon as they got organised. They did not wait long; they came at us at daybreak hoping to surprise us. Fail, the British Army has been 'standing to' at first light for hundreds of years so we were prepped and ready. They decided on a mass attack, thinking I suppose that they would overwhelm us. There were cars, trucks and even a bus, filling the road, with fighters running alongside brandishing and firing their AK 47's, most of them making the usual AK mistake of firing on full auto which means you run out of bullets pretty quickly.

I started shouting instructions at the guys until Tommo interrupted,

'Sarge' he said,

'We got this, this is what we do, if I need a truck fixing, I will call you, yeah?'

OK I thought, bit harsh on the truck fixing comment but never mind, go for it, so I shut the F! up.

He started shouting commands to the guys, most of which I didn't hear.

Suddenly four of the tubes were firing, two, three then four bombs from each. I watched the road and saw that the bombs were dropping in a line across the ridge on the road that led back down to the estate, to be fair they were blowing the shit out of the militants on the ridge line but not doing much for the runners and vehicles closing in on our position.

Then the other two tubes came in, I watched fascinated as they started dropping bombs from the ridge back towards the nick, splatting all the vehicles and people who were now trapped between the ridge and the building, they were using a mixture of anti-personnel and 'Willy Pete', the deadly white phosphorous bombs that burn everything they touch.

There was chaos, exactly what Tommo intended, I leaned over the parapet and started firing aimed single shots at specific individuals in the mass of attackers. I had been in combat before and I had learned that 'spraying and praying' on full auto had very poor results and that as I was a pretty good shot, I could usually hit what I fired at.

It always amused me to see those firefights on the tv in some cop drama or Hollywood movie when the good guys and the bad guys exchange millions of shots from their weapons, (without ever reloading,) at a distance of about fifty metres and very few people get hurt.

With my personal SA80 assault rifle I can hit a playing card at three hundred metres, I know this because that's how we used to practice when I was in the shooting team.

I had also learned in combat that most people fire their weapons too high and on automatic will run out of rounds in a few seconds, so if you can stay cool and fire single aimed shots you have a much better chance of a beer in the mess that evening.

The enemy were bunched up directly below us near the big door and Tommo yelled,

'Grenades, willy-pete,'

The guys left the tubes and taking grenades from the boxes by the parapet, began pulling the pins and dropping them over the edge. Nowhere to hide for the bad guys. Excellent!

The survivors then started running back towards the estate, occasionally some brave soul would turn towards us and unleash a full magazine of rounds after which I usually shot him. I then started picking off the retreating militants, shooting them in the right shoulder, yes, I am that good, as they ran.

Very difficult to shoot a rifle with a damaged shoulder and an injured man takes a lot of resources to look after, more than a dead one anyway. Yes I know it's not cricket but then we weren't playing cricket were we and I had a bunch of civilians and troops in my care who came first, sorry.

I had a shitty childhood, so when I joined the army, I was very grateful. Food, clothes, money, mates, a great job playing with motors and somewhere to live were all aspects of military life that I appreciated. This gave me what some people thought was a strange attitude.

There is an old military saying that 'a soldier never volunteers for anything', well I volunteered for everything. Courses, adventure training, deployments to places that would come last on any list of the twenty thousand places to see before you die. Everything. The thing was I had been to some amazing places and met some amazing people.

I was once on a 'jolly', that no one else wanted, in a country in Africa which shall remain nameless, firstly, because we weren't supposed to be there and secondly, because it's probably named something else now anyway. I was working with some vehicle guys from the French Foreign Legion, fantastic bunch of soldiers, I improved my spoken French no end.

They had been out there a while and had found that the local tribesmen often took two or three shots before they dropped as they had been chewing some kind of local weed that made them immune to pain.

The Legionnaires had found that the best way to deal with this was to shoot them in the throat if they were running towards you and in the shoulder as they were running away.

Thing with modern weapons is that they fire high velocity rounds, they don't just make a neat hole going through an enemy, they make a neat hole going in and a bloody big one going out. Hit someone anywhere in the throat and they went down, no matter how much weed they had chewed, or smoked or whatever they did with it. So that was my plan for all combat situations, and it had served me well.

Finally, there was nothing moving in the street just some burning vehicles and the horrible smell that you get when you mix white phosphorous with human flesh.

'Good job' I said to Tommo,

'Yes, they set themselves up really, giving us a kill zone'

'You know that they will be back,'

'Yes, but we will be ready, only two ways we lose this'

I had heard this saying before, but I decided to play along.

'What two ways?'

'Either we die, or we give up.' He said smiling,

I smiled as well and joined him in the punch line,

'And we aren't fucking giving up'

We stood the guys down then apart from two sentries watching the approaches to the building. They sorted out their kit and ammo states ready for the next contact. Setting up rest areas for the standby team who would stay on the roof to back up the sentries. I again checked with the radio guy, but he had no contact with anyone. All of our comms were still down and we were on our own.

2.

Later that afternoon I went back to the 4th floor where Lisa had set up her office. She was a very attractive woman, early 30s I think, shoulder length blonde hair and a really nice figure, well-hidden in a dark blue business suit. She also had 'the look', a sexy little twinkle in her eyes, not all women have it but the male readers will know what I mean. It's a look that says, 'anything is possible in the right circumstances,' mind you I had been wrong so many times about that in the past.

'I need to talk to you' she said, 'there is no way I am going to be captured by the militants, I have heard what they do to white women',

'What can I do?' I said,

'I want you to promise me that if we're going to be overrun you will shoot me in the head'.

I could understand this as I have served in some very dodgy areas of the world and my rule, also known in the military as 'Afghan Rules', is always that the last bullet was going in my mouth, so I get where she was coming from.

'I could do that' I said 'but I would need something from you in return'

I was seeing a slight opportunity here and had nothing to lose at this stage.

'What?' she said,

'I want to play with your tits,' I said,

'What?'

'I haven't touched a woman for months, and I might be dead tonight, so I want to play with your tits if you want me to shoot you in the head.'

She went very quiet for a minute or two, 'OK' she said. I turned back and locked the door. I slowly undid the buttons on her jacket and took it off.

She was standing at the end of the desk leaning on it, I put my left arm around waist and very slowly brought my right hand up to stroke her left breast. I tried to kiss her, but she turned her head away, OK I thought.

Her tits felt amazing, they were a really good size. I played with both of them for a few minutes then started to undo the buttons on her blouse.

'What are you doing?'

'You said I could play with your tits, so I want to play with them properly.'

She didn't say anything, but she didn't stop me either.

I managed to undo the blouse and slip it off over her shoulders. She was wearing a pink lacy bra that looked amazing. Stroking her tits over her bra felt fabulous so I reached around her back with both hands to undo the clasp,

'Hey' she said,

But I did it anyway pulling the bra away from her I was able to touch her naked breasts noticing that her nipples were very hard. I started to kiss them whilst I was stroking them and then started licking her nipples with my tongue.

'I never agreed to this bit' she said,

I ignored her. Her breathing was getting heavy by this stage and I noticed that her trousers were the soft silk type and very clingy. I undid the button at the front, pulled down the zip and they fell down to the floor. She was wearing very sexy pink knickers, I'd heard about this, women who wear severe looking business clothing wearing sexy underwear underneath wow!

She was breathing heavily now, I could smell the warm musky smell of an aroused woman,

'Let's get these knickers off'

'No' she said very softly,

I didn't think it was a real 'no' but to be honest I didn't really care. I slipped my hand around the waistband pulled them down and over her bum. They joined her trousers on the floor, and I put my hand between her legs and cupped her pussy. She was breathing heavily now, leaning her head against my shoulder, I slipped my finger into her pussy and found that she was very, very wet.

I slipped two fingers into the wetness and moved them up to her clitoris. Yes, surprise, I do know how to find a clitoris, it's not rocket science. No really, I had been on a course once and ended up sleeping with a Naafi manageress who was quite a bit older than me. She taught me some stuff in the bedroom which has served me well ever since. I gently played with her clit until her hips started twitching, usually a good sign so with my other hand I undid my trousers and got my dick out.

'Condom' she said,

Well that was lucky I thought as I had a pocket full of condoms, not as you might think because I was expecting to get lucky, but because they were the best thing to keep the rain out of your rifle barrel, stopped you getting a rusty bore!

I tore the packet open with my teeth and managed to slip it on with one hand whilst still stroking her pussy and clit with the other. I moved my body between her legs with my cock rubbing on her stomach. She was moaning now with both arms around my neck. I took hold of her hips and pulled her slowly to the edge of the desk and managed to slip inside her.

She was moaning softly now 'no, no, no, no'.

It felt amazing, I'd gone from being terrified a few hours ago, to feeling safer when we reached the nick and now, I was having sex with a very beautiful woman on her desk. I came very quickly I was so excited, I held her tightly when I stopped thrusting.

'Get out' she said,

I didn't know if she meant her pussy or the room, so I pulled out, zipped up my trousers and went to the door,

'Thank you' I said,

'Get out'

3.

We were two days in, they had hit us four times but so far, we were winning. The street leading up to the nick was full of bodies and the smell was appalling. Not my problem as none of the bodies were my guys.

We had no casualties and basically, we had shot the shit out of them. I was sitting having a coffee with my back to the far wall when the sentry, whose name I had forgotten, yelled 'Movement' in his broad Geordie accent, I'm sorry but it sounded like he was either shouting abuse or throwing up.

I walked up to the front parapet and Tommo joined me. I saw a guy walking down the hill towards us waving a white flag. He was wearing the usual flowing white robes and looked to be seriously overweight. I grabbed one of the big sniper rifles and sighted in on his chest.

'He's got a white flag,' Tommo said, 'He wants to talk to us.'

I was beginning to realise that although these guys were front line combat troops, they had trained for Germany and the European battle zone, they had never been deployed in some of the dodgy areas I had fought in. When you are in some hot dusty shithole, even if you are a vehicle specialist like me, then you 'Pick up a rifle and stand a post', as Jack Nicholson's character in 'A Few Good Men' used to say.

'Watch and learn' I told him, 'this guy is a suicide bomber if he gets close enough, we could be in trouble,'.

Depending on the type of explosives he was carrying he might have been able to damage the front wall of the building and the roller door mechanism which would have given us a real problem.

I peered through the telescopic sights and when he was about 400 metres away, I fired. I ducked down behind the parapet and waited for the explosion, it never came-shit!

I looked back and saw that he was just lying face up on the floor with a big pool of blood on the front of his robe.

'Guess he was just a fat fucker' one of the guys said.

Yes well I thought, I did not want to talk to them anyway. Fuck them if they can't take a joke.

The next event was about half an hour later, an ambulance pulled up at the top of the hill and a young white woman in a paramedic uniform came walking down the slope carrying a medical kit. She's brave I thought, we have just shot a guy with a white flag and she's out here with no cover.

Then the old paranoia kicked in, I had seen them use kids, donkeys, pregnant women, women with prams and once, an old fridge on a wheeled cart, as suicide bombs and I could imagine just how many fighters were in the back of the ambulance waiting to surprise us.   Not on my watch thanks.

Grabbing the rifle again I put two rounds through the front grille of the ambulance producing instant clouds of steam, I then shot out the front tyres.

Florence Nightingale had by this time finished checking the corpse and was standing looking at the wreckage of her vehicle. She turned towards us and gave us the middle finger with both hands, she was shouting something but fortunately we were too far away to hear it. Again, brave girl, I thought.

She picked up her kit and trudged back over the ridge line grabbing what looked like some paperwork out of the ambulance as she walked past it.

When she was well out of the way I shouted,

'Someone drop me a round on that ambulance please'.

Tommo translated that into mortar man speak and there was a crump as a bomb left the tube. Couple of seconds later there was a direct hit through the roof of the ambulance and a loud explosion. I expected to see bodies all over the place as the bad guys were blown apart but no, no one in the ambulance, shit, got that wrong as well. Still at least they knew now that we weren't going to fall for any tricks.

It was later that evening that Tommo came and sat down beside me on the roof.

'How are the guys doing?' I asked.

I had learned hard way that morale and discipline is very important in any combat situation. You need to keep the troops fed and watered, make sure that they have some downtime and also try to keep them busy. Idle hands etc.

'OK so far, we have not been in the shit like this before but they seem to think that you have, knowing about suicide bombers and stuff.'

'Yes, I have done Afghan and Iraq and some other shitholes I can't talk about, everybody needs vehicles and if you have vehicles then you need somebody like me, and if I'm there then I'm fighting.'

'We have mainly been with a training battalion at the depot, exercises in Germany and joint stuff in bits of Europe but nothing like this.'

'Yes, its scary shit for sure, if they get through that big door then we will have a real problem getting them out.'

We chatted a bit more about places we had served and then he said,

'Have you heard about the library downstairs?'

'No, not a big reader'

'No it's not about reading, some of the women have set it up as a knocking shop'.

Well that was new one on me, the last thing you could usually expect in a battlezone was a shag. I know I was making my own arrangements but I wasn't sure that Lisa would want me to share that information?

'How do you mean?'

'There are two doors into the library, so the guys queue up outside and the women go in from the other door. Each woman will do two guys, one at a time, and then they swap over.'

'Are they charging then?'

'No its not for money, they said they are grateful that we are fighting for them so it's their way of supporting the lads.'

'Wow,'

'So if you want a shag just go and queue up with the lads, 8-9 when the kids are settled for the night.'

'Can you choose?'

'No, it's the luck of the draw, there are a couple of Milfs in there and a couple of chunky monkeys but hey a shag's a shag yes?'

Well, yes it is but I think I would stick to my system for now although if she got any more grumpy then at least I had an option.

This library system was very unusual in my experience but I think it was mainly down to the fact that none of us expected to survive this. We had no chance of breaking out of this building so here we would have to stay.

4.

I was having a coffee downstairs when one of the troopers came running in,

'Sarge, sarge we got a sniper in the clock tower,'

Shit, this was the only place we were vulnerable, the clock tower of the town hall. It stuck up about forty metres above the roof of our building and we had very limited cover from that angle, crap!

I followed him back up the stairs and carefully crawled out onto the roof in the cover of the parapet. Tommo was hiding in the same place, he had brought a GPMG, but was not getting the chance to use it. Fuck.

I yelled to him,

'If I get his position, can you suppress him with the Gympy, long enough to get a couple of bombs up his arse?'

'Yes, but how are you going to do that?'

'Ready on three,' I yelled,

He nodded,

'One, two, three.'

I then set off running across the roof at an angle, snipers don't like angles, they prefer that you run away from them in a straight line so that they can shoot you, but I had seen this happen before. I mentally went through the aiming sequence in my head and suddenly reversed direction just as the shot arrived where I had been, I then carried on the same way and again counted out the seconds in my head, before leaping even further in the direction I was going, counting on the double bluff to get him to fire behind me which he did, result. Then I heard the Gympy start up and Tommo began shouting instructions to the team.

I rolled onto my back and saw the tracer rounds from the Gympy striking just below the clock face, Tommo was firing in short bursts which was keeping the twats head down until the mortar team started up. Other lads were firing their rifles at the same spot and then I heard the crump as the first round lifted off.

It smashed into the top of the clock face bringing shouts of derision about the accuracy from the other mortar crews, they quickly corrected and a couple of H.E. (high explosive) rounds blew the shit out of the tower. The spire started leaning outwards and as more rounds arrived it fell off and into the car park.

'Cease fire,' Tommo yelled above the noise, he then started adding instructions to the crew who altered their sights and fired again. This time dropping a bomb directly down into the tower through its gaping roof.

'Excellent' he said,

He then ordered a mix of armour piercing and white phosphorous rounds and the tower just vanished in a haze of dust and flame. Apparently, the AP rounds blew holes in the girders and beams, whilst the 'willy pete' rounds did what they do best which is set fire to everything they touch.

'Tommo, lose the rest of the building'

He nodded and brought a few more of the tubes into action. Soon bombs were smashing through the slate roof of the town hall and I could see the flames through the windows before they blew outwards from the explosives. I'm not leaving anywhere to be attacked from, I thought, and it will teach them a lesson.

No, I wasn't being brave in getting the snipers location, there are times in any combat situation when you just have to go for it, a sort of momentum builds up and if you take the view that you are dead anyway, then it means that you can sometimes get away with it, just as we had this time.

I had seen snipers in action, they are all cowards who would shit themselves fighting up close with other soldiers but are happy to terrorise opposition troops from a long distance away. Just hope he died slowly and painfully, preferably burning from the white phos. Bastard.

About twenty minutes later a fire engine arrived, stopped in front of the main building and a bunch of firepersons, started spraying water onto what was left of the ruins. This pissed me off in two ways, firstly, I had worked very hard to set that building on fire, risking life and limb and secondly, did they not get the message with the ambulance, dickheads?

Yes, I knew they were called 'firepersons' as I had been on one of those 'valuing diversity' courses (I volunteered-ha). It consisted of some pasty-faced captain from the education corps showing us a PowerPoint list of words we are not allowed to say anymore. It became a lot funnier when one of the scousers in the class, who was not a volunteer, began asking him to explain some of the more outrageous words and why they were now forbidden- hysterical!

I went to the weapons pile and picked up one of the big Accuracy International sniper rifles. Yes, I know I said I didn't like snipers, but I wasn't talking about me, was I? I walked to the parapet overlooking the town hall,

'Sarge, they are firemen.' Tommo said.

'Firepersons I think you will find Corporal Thompson,' I replied, in my best, 'taking the piss out of an officer', type voice.

'Anyway, don't stress I am just going to shoot the motor'

Vehicles are my business so my first couple of shots smashed the water pump powering the hoses and my second two punctured the water tank rendering the big red truck a bit useless. Fireman Sam would have been gutted. I shot out the tyres on my side so they could not drive it away.

I have the greatest respect for the bravery of firepersons, anyone who runs into burning buildings for a living can have my vote anytime, however, they were interfering with my battleground and I had the gun, so there. Yes, I know it's not a 'gun' because it has a rifled barrel, but I am trying to make this story interesting.

By this time, the FP's had gathered on the other side of the fire engine taking cover. Then one of them leaned around the back of the vehicle waving what looked like a white t-shirt.

'Oh shit,' said Tommo, 'they have got a white flag, please don't shoot them sarge.'

'OK, but when did we become, the National Trust?' I said.

Not sure why I picked the National Trust as an example, I suppose they were the least aggressive organisation I could think of at the time.

I wasn't going to shoot the FP's anyway; I had learned my lesson with the last bloke. They slowly trooped off around the back of the town hall and out of sight.

'Can somebody bomb me that fire engine please'

I looked around and saw that the mortar crews were looking at Tommo.

He nodded and two of them fired. Fireman Sam's favourite ride disappeared in a cloud of smoke.

Not sure about this, I could sense a bit of resentment building up. These guys were a very tight unit and they had suddenly been thrust under the command of someone who had never even fired a mortar. That was one course I hadn't been on.

The problem that could arise in the future is that if I gave a command that Tommo did not support, I might be left waving my dick at the enemy instead of raining mortar bombs down on their heads. Good job I had kept the platoon commanders Browning pistol when he had been killed. I wore it in a holster around my waist like an old-time cowboy. Interestingly, I was a crap shot with a pistol, sergeants don't usually have them issued so I had never practiced. Still if the shit truly hit the fan, I could shoot someone standing in front of me if I had to.

Everything on the roof was settling down now. The town hall was still smouldering, and the fire engine was burning nicely, ironic really, but this was war.

I left Tommo to sort out ammo states and food for the troops and wandered downstairs.

5.

Time to make my evening visit to Lisa.

'What do you want?' she asked, not very cheerfully, as I leaned around the doorway into her office.

'Just wondered if you wanted to renew our arrangement for another couple of days?'

'What do you mean?'

'Well, we had an arrangement involving me promising to shoot you and you letting me play with your lady bits.' Smooth eh?

'Are you saying that if I don't let you play with my tits you won't shoot me if we are being overrun?'

'Not at all, I'm saying if you don't have sex with me, I won't shoot you anywhere.'

'That's outrageous,'

'True but have you seen what they do to gorgeous blonde white women prisoners, you would be the entertainment for all of the young warriors,'

'Fuck off'

'OK, see you later,'

I walked to the door,

'Wait'

'If I agree this time then it counts for the rest of the time we are here.'

'No chance, two days per shag, take it or leave it.' I know, I know, I have never had any success with women because I never had anything to trade before. Just like with the sniper I was in locked down combat mode now where I just had to keep on going forward on the basis that I could be dead tomorrow, or even tonight.

'All right, but I'm not happy'

There were so many jokes I could have made about me not caring if she was happy or not as long as she had her knickers off and her legs open, but I thought that I had better not push it. Not if there's a chance of a shag.

I turned and locked the door, she stood up and came around to the end of the desk where I had enjoyed so much success just two nights ago. She was looking down at the ground, I leaned in to kiss her and she turned away,

'Don't kiss me',

OK I thought, suit yourself.

I undid her trousers and they slipped down to the ground. I reached into the waistband of her knickers and slowly slid them down around her bum, which was magnificent by the way, and off. I tried to turn her so that she was leaning on the desk,

'No,' she said, 'if you are going to fuck me then you fuck me to my face.'

Well I had never heard such language, actually I had, but this was really turning me on.

OK, I leaned her back on the desk and pulled her legs up. I stood between them and slipped my hand down to her pussy, which was very wet. Ah ha I thought, someone is more aroused than she is pretending to be, maybe she likes a little game of hide the sausage? (Yes, you can understand why I had very little success with women)

'Condom' she said,

'Or what?'

'Or you can make your own fucking arrangements Romeo,'

'Condom it is,'

I still had a goodly supply as it had not rained for a while. Shit, that would be a tough decision, if you were down to your last johnny, have a wet pussy or a wet rifle, let me think about it.

I moved in and pushed my cock into her, I loved the smell of an aroused woman and also the bit at the start when you have to push hard until you are in properly, then I loved the rest of it. I don't know if it was exhaustion or the sniper or what, but I had about six strokes and then came, it was amazing.

'Get out'

'Not yet',

I held her for a couple of minutes until I had subsided. She didn't protest and I felt really good. I leaned back out of her and she closed her legs whilst I fastened my trousers.

'Get out'

'I am out, can't you tell'

I swear that a glimmer of a smile crossed her face but then she was back in grumpy mode, it's a good job she was gorgeous with great tits and a wet pussy or I might have taken my business elsewhere.

'See you in a couple of days,'

'Don't hold your breath, I am due for my period'

'We will just have to be creative then'

I wasn't sure where this sparkling repartee was coming from, but I was impressing myself.

'Fuck right off.'

So, I did.

6.

I heard the noise I was hoping not to hear anytime soon, shit! There is nothing else in the world that sounds like it and it scares the crap out of me.

I ran to the back of the roof to where the noise was coming from behind the town hall ruins.

Tommo came and stood beside me,

'What's that noise?

'Armour.'

'Fuck,' he said

Fuck indeed young corporal I thought, they were not supposed to have any armoured vehicles but the noise of what sounded like a very heavy tracked vehicle was coming slowly towards us. I suppose it could be a bulldozer but no, not really, I knew that noise. I listened very carefully and to me it sounded like a main battle tank. Shit!

They weren't supposed to have any tanks but I guess that if they had captured one and they had some ex-army guys in their ranks then they might just have been able to move it and more importantly fire its main armament.

At this distance it could just sit there and destroy the police station and us in it. But, they could also have done that from a kilometre away, out of our sight, maybe that meant that they didn't know how to work the complicated optical systems to fire the main gun remotely and were just planning to show up and point and shoot.

'Get some AP rounds set up please' I told Tommo.

Armour piercing mortar rounds sound like a good idea but in reality, it was very hard to damage a tank with a mortar round as all of the sloping surfaces on the turret and body of the tank let the bombs slide off before detonating. The only real aiming point would be the flat engine covers at the back and the small area around the drivers hatch at the front

Tommo was shouting at the guys and they were standing by all of the tubes. I grabbed a gimpy and some ammo belts and set up on the parapet facing the source of the noise. The tank would have to come around the building and stop so that they could line up the gun, we would have a very tiny time window in which to do whatever we could to stop them.

The front of the tank started poking out from behind the building, shit, Challenger one, it was an older type of tank but very, very effective in its day. This one looked battered and broken so I wondered if it had been abandoned after another battle and they had managed to get it going again. Not good.

It came lumbering around the building, fortunately for us the main gun was pointing low and to the left, I was hoping they had a problem with it, but no, just as I thought that it started traversing across and upwards heading in our direction.

'Anytime you are ready corporal' I yelled, wondering why he had waited this long?

I started aiming the GPMG at the barrel of the tank, I had once heard about someone firing rounds directly down a tank barrel and whilst the tank ammo did not explode it did jam the gun and stopped it firing. I didn't really have any other options at that point.

I heard the tubes firing, they only fired one round each and I wondered why until I realised that Tommo was sighting them in on the target. Good practice I suppose but I would have preferred them to drop dozens of rounds on the fucker, making it very noisy inside and hopefully putting them off.

As usual he was right and I was wrong because four of the bombs missed the tank altogether. The good news was that three of them didn't, two smashing into the engine covers and one dropping right on top of the driver's hatch, outstanding.

The big gun was still swinging towards us and I opened up with the Gympy firing a full two hundred round belt at the gaping hole in the barrel. Some of the rounds were hitting it and some weren't. Then I saw what I had been hoping for, the drivers hatch was starting to lift as he either panicked or had to get out because of damage inside the vehicle. Bingo. As the driver poked his head out, I fired another burst and splatted him, that meant that the Challenger was now a sitting target, literally. Excellent. Then I had another idea.

'Willy-pete,' I yelled

The bombs were away in seconds and I stood back to watch.

We didn't actually work with heavy armour in my trade, but I had done courses with tankies and spent many a happy hour at the Tank Museum. What do tankies fear most of all? Think about it, you drive around all day in a sixty-ton, heavily armoured behemoth with a massive gun, what are you most scared of? Fire. The inside of a tank is a nightmare of fittings and kit, none of which is designed for the comfort of the crew. If it catches fire, it's a terrible place to get out of. Hence the willy-pete command to the boys.

This time five of the bombs hit, spreading their deadly white phosphorous all over the vehicle. The stuff sticks where it hits and the tank was engulfed in flames and smoke, I saw the commanders hatch lift slightly, so I put a burst of rounds onto it. It was facing away from me unlike the drivers hatch so I couldn't fire directly into it, but that left the tank crew with a terrible decision. Climb out and get shot or stay in and fry. Nightmare.

Then the ammo cooked off, Shit. There was a massive explosion and the turret burst open. The crew were all dead by this point and then some of the other ammo started cooking off and we all hunkered down behind the parapet for safety. That would have been ironic, getting hit by ammo that was exploding in a tank we had just killed. Not sure why we were giggling but we were. Result.

7.

'Oh shit, oh shit, oh shit, you need to see this boss,'

The sentry was babbling as if he was in shock, they had started calling me 'boss' which I didn't mind but I didn't want them to get too familiar, they still needed to jump when I said so.

I went over to where he was standing and looked down on the approach road, and shit, I could see what he meant.

There was a bunch of about half a dozen militants coming towards us, they stopped about five hundred metres away, just outside the effective range of our SA80's. One of them was brandishing a big sword and more worryingly one of them was dragging Florence Nightingale, the paramedic along with him. One was carrying a tripod with a camera on and they were all wearing face masks and body armour, shit, shit, shit.

Florence's hands were tied behind her back and she was stumbling along as if in shock. I had seen crap like this before but only on video.

'Stand to' I yelled, and all the guys who had been dozing on the roof came awake and grabbed their rifles, I grabbed the big rifle I had used on the fire engine and watched the proceedings through the telescopic weapon sight.

They dragged Florence to the middle of the street and the guy with the sword or 'Fuckwit the Executioner' as we started calling him, was shouting and waving the sword in the air. The militant with the camera was setting it up facing Fuckwit and Florence, they were going to behead her. They forced Florence to her knees, and he stood behind her still shouting. Fuck.

Not on my watch I thought, I sighted in on her with the rifle, I had a clear view of her face, her head was directly in front of his stomach so the round would go through her and him without slowing down much at this range. This would leave her dead and him gutshot, it would take him a long time to die then as I would personally shoot the shit out of anyone who tried to help him. Then I saw her eyes.

Time for Plan B.

'Sight on the militants, I have the guy with the sword, aim at the tops of their heads and fire a burst, call out from the left,'

The guys checked in, so I knew that all of the other five baddies were now covered,

'Fire on my shot'

I sighted in on the body armour chest plate of Fuckwit and gently squeezed the trigger. Bingo, the bullet knocked him flat on his back and Florence fell forwards onto her face. I heard the other rifles firing and hoped that aiming at the tops of their heads would allow for the bullet drop over that distance and that at least some of the rounds would hit their targets, if not I would be in the shit with plan B.

'Tommo get me some smoke out'

I placed the rifle carefully on the ground and ran to the 'Escape System' case I had opened earlier. Flicking the lid open, I grabbed the metal bar and hurled it over the edge of the roof with the rope trailing after it. Shoving on some gloves, I leaned over the edge, grabbed the rope and threw myself off the roof. Crazy, you might think but not really, you just have to keep going forwards in a firefight so I was. Anyway, I had done some fast roping and mountain climbing in other places on the globe so I knew I could hold my bodyweight and control my descent with the gloves.

In what seemed like a couple of seconds I was slowing myself down with my hands and boots and then bending my knees for the landing. I turned and sprinted to where the group of bad guys were. They were all down, the 'top of the head' aiming point trick had worked a treat. A couple of bombs landed on the far side of the group and thick orange smoke was masking the view of the enemy at the top of the hill.

Fuckwit was holding his chest and struggling to breathe when I got there so I picked up the sword with both hands, found it to be surprisingly heavy, waved it above my head and smashed it down on his throat. Wow, it was certainly sharp, going most of the way though his neck before getting stuck in what I assume was his spine. Blood was spurting everywhere. I couldn't pull it out so left it where it was, turned around and grabbed Florence by the middle of the back of her jumpsuit. She was making a weird crying noise, hardly surprising, I picked her up, spun her around, threw her over my shoulder and started running like hell back to the building.

We had trained for this, every year, battlefield casevac, casualty evacuation. I usually ended up with some chunky duvet technician, (a storeman, formerly known as a blanket stacker,) all his kit and his rifle, all my kit and my rifle as well, so to be fair a skinny paramedic was no bother at all really.

I started legging it back to the building, I could hear bullets whizzing past us as the militants fired into the smoke, then I heard some heavier bombs going off behind me and someone cut loose above us with the Gympy which was a big relief. I did a fair bit of running so I was ok with that bit of the plan but as I got closer to the building two things came to mind.

One, was that Florence has a really nice arse, I was holding it with my right hand to stop her bouncing up and down on my shoulder with no sexual motive whatsoever your honour. The male readers will know what I mean about this, most women have great arses when they are wearing heels but Florence was definitely a GAFS, (Great Arse in Flat Shoes,) and two, how the fuck was I going to get up that rope?

On my own I could probably climb up the five stories given time but I'm not sure Florence could, and I certainly couldn't carry her. As we got closer, I could hear shouting, I looked up and saw Tommo leaning over the parapet yelling,

'Grab the rope, grab the rope'

We reached the bottom of the rope and I managed to grab it with my arms around Florence and stood on the metal bar. We started going up as someone started pulling on the rope, slowly at first and then accelerating till we were travelling at the speed of a fairly fast lift. Shit, he must have had the regimental tug of war team on the end of that rope

We reached the top, Tommo was guiding the pullers and as soon as he could he reached over and took Florence from me, I squirrelled up another foot and pulled myself over the wall. Lying on the ground I was panting for breath wondering how the hell we had got away with that again.

Tommo cut the flexicuffs from Florence's wrists and she came walking over to where I was lying.

'Bastard,'

She yelled and started kicking me with her paramedic clogs.

'Why did you have to shoot him, he had a white flag, then you bombed my wagon, what the fuck?'

The guys who had been on the rope were falling about laughing at this until Tommo came up behind her, put his arm around her waist and lifted onto his hip.

'Come along now miss, leave the sergeant alone, let's get you cleaned up.'

It was just like a scene from one of those black and white Ealing comedies, Tommo sounded just like an old-style village copper. Even I could see the funny side.

'Nice work with the sword boss,' one of the guys said, 'thought we were in the cavalry'

I just grinned, I was too wasted to reply.

8.

Well, after I got my breath back, I was ready for another visit to Lisa, nothing like a quick brush with death to make you feel like a shag. I made my way down to her office, I knocked and went in, she came around the desk and stood in front of me.

'Did you go down a rope to get Isabelle?'

'Who?'

'The paramedic, her name is Isabelle.'

'Oh, you mean Florence, that's what we call her,'

'Her name is Isabelle.'

You know you can have these conversations with women that are totally pointless, but they don't think they are, well this appeared to be one of them.

'Yes, Isabelle, they were going to chop her head off,'

She pointed at a sofa in the corner of the office,

'Sit down,'

I sat down,

'Keep your hands to yourself and don't say anything'

WTF?, ok I thought.

She moved my legs apart and started to undo my trousers. I said nothing, holding my breath, she pulled them down to my ankles and then pulled the waistband of my boxers out and away from my cock. Promising. She eased my boxers down until they joined my trousers and then knelt down between my legs.

She reached out with her right hand and slowly cupped my balls, as her left hand began to stroke me, she leaned forward and kissed the end of my dick. Wow! Then she took me into her mouth, no condom, nothing. I know that there is no such thing as a bad blow job but this was amazing, she was gently squeezing my balls and stroking my shaft whilst moving her head up and down on me, her tongue licking and teasing me inside her mouth all at the same time.

I felt something happening,

'Can I come in your mouth?

She pulled her head back,

'That's the idea dickhead'

And started sucking me again,

Well even if it was grumpy blow job it was still the best blow job I had ever had, so I came straight away.

Surprisingly, she didn't run away retching but kept me in her mouth until I had finished twitching, then she carefully eased her head to one side letting my cock rest on my leg. Very classy. She wriggled back to her feet then went to the desk, picked up a tissue from a box and in a very ladylike way spat my come into it. Dropping it in the bin she reached out for her mug and took a drink, presumably to rinse her mouth. I was impressed, this woman was the real deal.

'That was amazing,'

'Don't get used to it, it's a special occasion.'

Fair enough, I sorted my pants out and went around to the end of the desk where she was standing. I put my arm round her waist and said,

'Thank you. I needed that'

She didn't push me away this time and when I looked at her face, I could see that she was crying. I put my other arm around her, and she just sagged into me, cuddling up like she had never done before.

'Are we going to die?'

What could I say, we kept winning the battles, but we had no way of knowing what was going on in the rest of the country? Anything I said now would be a mistake, so I said nothing.

She held me for a couple of minutes and then straightened up,

'Get out'

'No'

I took her hand and led her to the sofa I sat down pulling her down next to me and put my arm around her shoulder,

'Let's just sit for a while'. I said. So we did.

I was starting to have feelings for this woman and ever the opportunist I said,

'You know when this is over?'

She immediately put her finger on my lips to stop me speaking, ooh I thought I know where that finger has just been, but ever the gentleman, I didn't make a big deal of it.

'No,' she said, 'when this is over, if we survive you will never mention this to anyone ever again, do you understand?'

Obviously, she was having difficulty dealing with her feelings for me, I could understand this. The romantic assignations, the smell of cordite, the ever-present risk of death. Sounds like a movie.

'If you mention it to anyone, I will say that you raped me at gunpoint, and they will believe me not you.'

'Well to be accurate I raped you 'not at gunpoint' because my threat was that I wouldn't shoot you if you didn't screw my brains out.'

She thought about this and again I just caught a very vague hint of a smile before she said,

'Just don't tell anyone ok'

'OK'

It was going dark when I left and went back upstairs, she didn't seem to hate me as much now which I suppose was some kind of improvement. It was my turn for the early stag (sentry duty) whilst Tommo got some rest, he would come up about 12.30 and I would grab a snooze and be back up for first light about five o'clock. They hadn't hit us at dawn since day one but the British Army didn't get where it is today by sleeping through first light so we would stand to as usual.

I was sitting with my back to the parapet when Florence or rather Isabelle reappeared. Someone had found her a track suit to wear and she had loosened her hair from its ponytail, she was in fact looking good. She came towards me and I put my hands up saying,

'No, no don't hurt me again,'

'Funny' she said and sat down next to me.

'Thanks for coming to get me,'

'You're welcome, I wasn't going to let them execute you'

To be fair I wasn't, I was going to shoot her, still best not mention that.

We sat there in silence for a while and she said,

'Is there anything I can do to help?'

I thought for a minute, she was a fully trained paramedic far more useful than the 'stick a field dressing on it and hope for the best' school of battlefield medicine that we had been trained in.

I remembered that I had fallen off a motorcycle once on some off-road training, I had injured my leg and it was bleeding quite badly, I had drawn my Leatherman multitool with the blade out and threatened to stab anyone who came near me until the proper ambulance crew turned up, oh we did laugh.

'Yes, next time they are shooting at us you could come up here with some medical kit and just be on standby in case any of the guys gets hit.'

'Yes, I could do that' she said, 'I will just nip back to my ambulance and get my kit, oh wait a minute somebody blew it the fuck up.'

I pointed at the guys playing cards across the roof,

'One of them' I said, 'I'm not allowed to fire a mortar.'

'Yea right,' she smiled.

We sat there in silence again, then she said,

'Just one more thing, if you are ever wanting to visit the library, will you let me know?'

She looked directly into my eyes when she said it, so even I was in no doubt about what she meant. (Me being a lifetime-achievement award holder in the 'misunderstanding the subtle messages of women' awards-ongoing)

She left, accidentally giving me a great view of her arse in the flat shoes, or maybe deliberately, hard to tell with women.

9.

We had been here for five days and I was exhausted. None of us were sleeping very well and the idea of just sitting here whilst they attacked us day after day was doing my head in. The guys were starting to bicker amongst themselves and considering that they were all armed to the teeth, the prospect of some serious blue-on-blue action was getting closer all the time. (that's when you shoot someone from your own side either by design or accidentally, that's what we call it because there is no such thing as friendly fire)

It was about half-seven, Tommo should have gone for his nap, but he was still here on the roof with me. The only activity I could see was that the church about a kilometre away had the lights on.

'Quiet tonight,' I said

'Friday, it's when they all get together,'

Shit, yes, I had lost track of the days and it was Friday. They were all in one place.

I took a couple of deep breaths, I looked around at this rag tag bunch of heroes who had fought a tireless enemy to a standstill. Fuck it.

I drew my pistol and held it down by my side. Here we go then.

'All tubes,' I yelled,

I had been listening to Tommo when he was giving fire commands and although I couldn't do the accent, I knew enough of the words to manage.

Several of the guys looked at me but no one moved.

'Target half-left, church building, range one kilometre, two rounds armour piercing then two rounds high explosive,'

Significantly the only person who moved was a young trooper named Morgan, he came up to me and in a very shaky voice said,

'Sarge, sarge you cannot bomb a church, they are in there praying,'

I moved my weight onto my left heel and with my right hand backhanded him across the side of the head with the pistol. He went straight down; it was shit or bust now. I pointed the pistol at his head and clicked the safety catch off, it sounded very loud.

Tommo was at my side in a second, he did not make the mistake of grabbing my arm if he had I think I would have just flipped.

'Corporal Thompson, get this coward off my battleground, lock him up in one of the cells.'

Tommo dragged Morgan to his feet and helped him away from me, Morgan was just muttering to himself and he seemed a bit dazed. Fair enough.

'All tubes,' I repeated and cocked the pistol sending the round from the breech skidding across the roof. That noise seemed to break the spell because that was when they moved, grabbing bombs, adjusting the sights, and standing ready by the mortars.

I really, truthfully could not see any other way forward, we did not have a lot of ammunition left and the inevitable outcome would be that they would come at us and breach the big vehicle door. Then they would be in the building and the women and children would be taken. Not whilst I was breathing mate. It was as if the whole of my military career had led me to this point. Another deep breath.

'Fire,'

I may have mentioned it before, but these guys were fast. Within about five seconds there were twenty-eight bombs in the air. There was the usual short time lag and then they hit, pounding down through the roof of the church and blowing the living shit out of the building. Wow! As the dust cleared, I could see that the roof had gone, and the building had collapsed. No point stopping now.

'Two rounds willy-pete.'

I looked at the tubes and they were standing there with rounds in their hands ready to fire, finally they were listening to me.

'Fire'

It seemed to take forever but then we saw the dreadful white phosphorous bombs bursting onto the ruins of the building. Have some of that you wankers I thought.

Tommo had come back from sorting Morgan and he looked out and saw what I had done. I was ready for an argument, but he didn't say anything, we just stood there in silence watching the flames and smoke rising from the destroyed building.

'Stand the men down now Corporal, sort out their food and personal admin. Rest in sections and get me an ammo state please.'

It was very formal after the five days we have just had but I felt that our relationship would have to be very formal from now on. I had just taken that final, irrevocable step to total war.

I went downstairs and headed for Lisa's office, I needed the comfort of a woman now and I didn't fancy queueing up at the library. I walked into her office and saw her standing by the heavily shielded window looking out.

'Have you just bombed the church,'

'Yes,'

'Oh my god,'

She had moved back towards the desk and I turned her around and put her hands on the desk. Standing behind her I pulled her trousers and then her knickers down. She was trembling and shaking and the effect on her bum was very erotic.

I dropped my trousers and slipped a condom on. I took hold of her hips.

'Not in my bum,'

'No, in your pussy.'

I pushed her down onto the desk, leaned forward and entered her from behind. I think this is my favourite sexual position as you can reach their tits and enjoy the feel of their arse on your stomach.

It also lets them think about who they would rather be shagging than you.

I think I was a little out of my head at this stage, but it must have affected Lisa because she was thrusting back against me, matching me stroke for stroke. I thrust harder and harder into her; I was feeling invincible which I suppose was some sort of reaction to the stress of the battle.

'I'm coming' she said,

'I'm coming, I'm coming, I'm coming, Fuck me.'

She started twitching and writhing about beneath me and it was like the spell had broken and I shot my load and collapsed on her back. Wow!

Most of the women I had sex with had found it difficult to achieve orgasm whilst we were having sex and usually needed the attention of their small battery driven assistant to reach an outcome. Might be my technique I suppose, or lack of it?

Lisa was now sobbing and twitching on the desktop. I leaned back turned her around and just held her. She put her arms around me and hugged me really, really tightly.

'Bastard, bastard, bastard, I haven't done that since Max.'

Well, I was not sure if that was a complement or a criticism, but I decided to take the points anyway as the berserk warrior spell that had affected me was definitely broken now.

We hugged, she cried.

When our breathing had calmed down I stepped away to get dressed and she pulled her knickers and trousers up, as she fastened them she did that little hip wriggle that women do when they are getting dressed, I always enjoyed watching that.

'You know that they are going to destroy us now,'

'So what's changed, at least we have taken a few more of their players out of the game.'

She sat at her desk and went very quiet. After a few minutes, I just nodded to her and left the office.

10.

I was due to take the early slot for a rest and go back upstairs when the duty sentry woke me, usually about twelve-thirty. I had sorted my room out on the same floor as Lisa's office, away from where the lads were sleeping. Sort of a mini, sergeants mess I suppose but it also gave them some privacy.

I went to my room, locked the door and dragged a large table across the doorway to slow down anyone who was trying to enter. I was pretty sure that the troops would be pissed off after tonight and might decide to take matters into their own hands. I was not one of them so any unit integrity would work in favour of Tommo and trooper Morgan. Fuck them if they can't take a joke.

I arranged some pillows under the blankets on the bed to look as if it was occupied. I slept on the floor in the far corner of the room with my rifle set to automatic, ready to fire and with the safety catch off. My thinking was that by the time they had smashed their way in I could have the rifle up and be dispatching a number of rounds in their general direction. I had noticed the irony of the fact that I was now hiding from my own troops as well as the enemy-shit.

Bizarrely I slept. I woke up, checked my watch and saw it was seven in the morning, they had let me sleep through, fuck. I splashed some cold water on my face, clicked the safety catch on both of my weapons to safe and headed upstairs.

Tommo was standing on the roof watching the town with just one other sentry, wtf?

'Did we stand to?' I asked,

'No need, they have been busy all night, putting the fires out and carting away the bodies, I went down to one sentry at times as there was just nothing happening, thought you could do with the rest,'

'Fair enough, so no movement from the town then?'

'Not really I think they were all in the church'

'So, nothing then?'

'Maybe, from about two am we heard cars and buses and heavy vehicles arriving for about three hours, sounds like reinforcements, possibly hundreds of them,'

'Fuck,' I said,

'Fuck indeed,'

'Ammo state?'

'About fifty rounds of 5.56, a couple of belts for the gympys, and twenty-two bombs for the tubes. Eight grenades between us and that's it. We might slow down one more attack but that's all we can do.'

'Where have they parked all these motors then?'

He paused for a moment,

'Footy field at the far side of the estate?'

We had seen it on the local maps we had, it was the only place you could realistically park hundreds of vehicles.

'Probably, can you reach it with a tube?'

'We could, it's about two klicks, (kilometres) away but we can't see what we we're shooting at and I would sooner save the bombs for the next attack.'

Fair enough, he is the mortar guy after all, I just bomb churches.

'What about the Gympy?'

'What about it?'

'In the SF role'

'What's that?'

'SF -sustained fire, I saw it on a video once, you set it on the tripod and fire it upwards at forty-five degrees, the thing is the bullets don't all land in one place, they spread out to cover a really big area when they hit.'

'Don't you want to save the ammo for when they come?'

'Not really, I would sooner fuck with them while we can, grab me the maps please.'

I grabbed a Gympy, checked the case it came in and found a tripod. I set it up facing the village and put ten tracer rounds at the front of the belt. I pointed it up at forty-five degrees and waited for the map. Tommo came back and we spread the map out in front of us. We tinkered with the angle and when we were ready I fired a short burst. The rounds arced up into the sky and started dropping back to earth well past the houses. They looked to be going a bit far, so I pointed the barrel up to about sixty degrees and fired the rest of the belt.

'I'll save one belt for later,'

He nodded.

There was not much we could do after that. There was some food about, but I was too stressed to eat. We had had a good run and today looked like being the final day of the competition when the overall winner would be decided.

We were standing there listening when I heard the sounds of some big engines starting up, out of our sight beyond the estate. Then the unmistakeable noise of several heavy tracked vehicles moving through the streets. The guys were all on their feet now.

'Any ideas?' Tommo said.

'Just one,'

'Detail,' I yelled, they all looked at me, 'Fix bayonets,'

It's a drill you practice until you are bored shitless, but I suppose that is the point because they all obeyed the order without question. I fixed my bayonet onto my rifle being careful not to touch the blade. I knew it was razor sharp because we had grinding wheels in the workshop, it was also coated with a vehicle specific, anti-corrosion coating so that I didn't have to keep cleaning it.

They were all looking at me now, expecting words of wisdom and inspiration, yeah right.

'As soon as they appear, we fire whatever ammo we have left then Corporal Thompson will take half of you and guard the big door downstairs for as long as you can. The rest of you will come with me to the corridor outside the library, and we will fight to the death.'

I took a deep breath.

'Only two ways we lose this, we die, or we give up,'

As one voice they shouted,

'And we're not fucking giving up!'

I smiled, never gets old that one, never said it for real though. I suppose as a soldier you understand deep down that one day you might run out of luck or ammunition or both and that day was today. That's why you keep going forwards. I had a stray thought from a very old movie I had enjoyed years ago. I picked my rifle up by the grip held it over my head and yelled,

'No prisoners,'

They raised their rifles and yelled in unison,

'No prisoners,'

'Carry on Corporal'

Yes, I know you cannot order 'no prisoners' because it is against one of the four Geneva Conventions, well fuck that, because (a) we are not in Geneva and (b) we are not at a Convention so there. Yes, I was losing it, but so be it.

Shit, almost forgot about Lisa, I need to nip down to her office and slot her. I had thought it through, I would just walk straight into her office with my pistol down at my side then shoot her in the head before she had time to be afraid. Then I would put another round into her head whilst she lay on the floor to make sure. Needs must etc.

The guys were all in their firing positions, what was left of the ammo was laid out and I could see the grim expressions on their faces. There are worse places to die I thought, in my own country, fighting alongside some good lads, trying to save some women and children. Better than tripping an IED in some foreign shithole. Bring it on you bastards!

Then I heard the noise, I wasn't sure at first, I thought it might be my mind playing tricks but no, it was definitely the noise.

11.

I had heard the noise in many different, desperate combat situations in a number of very hot countries scattered around the world. As a vehicle specialist I always thought it sounded a bit grating, as if the engine was out of balance slightly but that's because it was a jet turbine engine, not a car engine, but more importantly it was the noise of the two jet turbine engines fitted to my second favourite helicopter, an Apache gunship.

And not just one Apache gunship but four, coming at us from the north, flying very low as they usually did to confuse any idiots on the ground who might be thinking of having a pop at them - not recommended. Wow! Three minutes later and I would have blown Lisa's brains all over the office, that would have required some fast talking and a lot of paperwork, perhaps I should have got her to sign a consent form to her being shot in case of capture. Yes, I was babbling now, the situation had just changed from a few squaddies with fixed bayonets and very little ammunition to a few squaddies with some very serious backup.

Of course, the lads had started singing 'Ride of the Valkyrie' from the helicopter sequence in 'Apocalypse Now', (and the Wagner opera-duh!), pretty much standard whenever you get pulled out of the shit by helicopters. Well I say singing, if you can imagine a bunch of stressed out, exhausted, largely tone-deaf Geordies giving it their best Wagner solos on the top of a bombed-out nick then you will know what I mean.

The Apaches split into two pairs, one pair peeling to our left towards the estate whilst the other two came straight over us, and flew beyond the town hall ruins, obviously intent on clearing the other side of the town centre. The pair that were over the estate started firing into the buildings having found some sort of targets.

I was becoming a little delirious now, shouting,

'Not so fucking hard now are you?' to the distantly assembled militants who could neither see nor hear me.

Suddenly the two Apaches over the estate spiralled up, one going left and one going right, firing distraction flares as they went, I had seen this happen before when helicopter gunships ran into some serious armoured opposition. I also knew what happened next. I looked hard to the north and caught sight of my all-time favourite aircraft.

Some people say they are ugly, trust me if you are on the ground, in trouble, and the Apaches can't sort it then this is what you want, the Grumman A10, the 'Tank buster'. A beautiful piece of kit. They fly so slowly you think they will fall out of the sky, but they are very, very effective. This one started firing its massive, depleted uranium shells at something on the ground and I could see the empty cases falling from the nose of the aircraft, somebody on the estate was now officially having a very bad day.

I had seen the A10 in action in a couple of HDS's (Hot dusty shitholes) and when they fired at a vehicle it just disappeared, I don't mean it was damaged, it just wasn't there anymore. The A10 cleared off and the Apaches fired a couple of times into the estate and then came back over the nick and started flying big lazy figure of eights. This is known in the business as 'top cover' and it exists so that something else can fly in underneath it, in safety.

I looked north again, and this time saw my very favourite helicopter, the Chinook, a bunch of them in fact. The Chinook got the vote over the Apache every time because I could get a lift to safety in the back of a Chinook and there was no passenger space on the Apache, ha ha!

The other two Apaches had flown back around the town hall ruins down over the car park at the side of the nick and had started to hover about twenty feet off the ground facing the town hall. Then bedlam erupted, they fired all of their Hellfire missiles and rockets and endless rounds of cannon ammunition at the ruins. They were clearing the area for an opposed landing; I could have told them that there was nothing moving in the ruins, but they didn't ask me. They flew off to the east as the first of the Chinooks came in, flaring out to land with the tail ramp coming down.

Three land rovers reversed rapidly out of the back crammed with troops, they drove to the exits of the square and the guys piled out to set up a defensive perimeter. Shit, even from a distance I could recognize the unit badges, this was the 'Maroon Machine', paras, soldiers from the Parachute

Regiment, I almost felt sorry for the wankers in the village, almost.

I had worked with the Paras before and whilst you don't want to be in a bar with them at kicking out time, if you were ever truly in the shit, and we had been, then these were the guys you wanted pouring out of the choppers to help you out.

The Chinooks were landing thick and fast now, troops pouring out onto the car park, two of the aircraft had Jackal armoured vehicles slung beneath them and these were crewed up and sent off towards the village where I would imagine that a lot of the previously gun-toting, super aggressive assholes would be dressing in their wife's clothing and trying to make good their escape, fat chance.

'Detail', I yelled, the guys looked at me in surprise,

'Unfix bayonets, or whatever the fuck the command is.'

I had never given the command to fix bayonets, so I wasn't sure what the unfix command was, they got the message however and turned their weapons back from sharp, pointy sticks into rifles again. I then had my second brainwave.

'Detail- unload'

I had not always been popular with this bunch and I had a sudden worry that a stray round might end up in my back during the chaos of the wind-down.

The guys stripped the magazines off and cleared their rifles holding them open for inspection. I had a quick check of all of the breeches making sure there were no random rounds lying about that might have had my name on.

'Make safe' I yelled, this meant that they put the magazines back on the weapons but would have to cock them again before they could fire.

My rifle wasn't made safe and neither was my pistol so if I heard a noise, I didn't like I would just slip the safety catch off and I would be ready to rock and roll.

Tommo was at my shoulder, 'Trooper Morgan' he said,

'Get him out, tell him and the lads to keep their mouths shut and we are all good.'

'Cheers,' He vanished,

'OK guys let's go catch a ride out of here, the first beers are on me,'

That got a reaction and the guys started moving towards the stairs.

When they had left, I stood on the roof on my own just breathing it in, the smell of aviation fuel and cordite from the missiles being very, very welcome.

I knew I would get the shakes later as I always did after a firefight, but I also knew that it would be when I was finally on my own and not before.

I went slowly down the stairs and out onto the car park, the women and children were being shepherded into a chopper, I tried to catch Lisa's eye, but she was busy, or ignoring me which amounted to the same thing really.

A land rover was parked in the middle of the square with a young-looking para captain talking to a couple of his guys. I walked over to him to give him my report, hoping that I could then GTF out of here. I didn't salute him, you don't salute officers on a battleground as there may be a sniper watching, unless of course the officer is a total asshole in which case you do salute him and hope that there is a sniper watching, pisses them off no end.

'Sorry we are a bit late to the party sarge,' he said, 'it's been a bit hectic elsewhere.'

'No worries boss, you arrived just in time, thanks.'

'Did you really fix bayonets?'

'Yes, the ammo was running out, so we were going to get up close and personal with them'

'Outstanding!' he said.

The Chinook with the kids on was spooling up and the guys were waving goodbye to the 'library' staff as it lifted off. Two of the Apaches followed it out of the car park, one leading the way and one flying higher up behind it. Any nutcase on the ground with an RPG would be well advised to pick another target rather than tackle this precious cargo.

I started to relax a bit now, it looked like we had got away with it. The lads were standing around chatting and as usual with their accents I was getting about one word in three but never mind, we would soon be out of here whilst the paras dished out a bit of local retribution.

The last Chinook had dropped off its troops when three differently dressed guys came out of the back. Similar headgear to the paras but not really as welcome, these were redcaps, Military Police, a CSM (Company Sergeant-Major) and two sergeants and as usual they were massive blokes, all built like brick shithouses.

Like most squaddies I had experienced a few run ins with the MP's usually when alcohol had been involved, I had always lost the fights but gained a healthy respect for them (and avoided them as much as possible). I assumed that they had come to take command of the building but not so.

They marched up to where we were standing and came to a very smart halt. I did think of saluting the CSM just in case there were any snipers handy but you don't salute warrant officers anyway so I would have just looked like a prick.

'Sergeant Michael Lewis,' the CSM said, 'You are under arrest on suspicion of murder and war crimes.'

Fuck me I wasn't expecting that.

'Put your weapons on the ground'

So, I did, working really on automatic now as I tried to comprehend what was happening. I put my rifle and pistol down on the floor. One of the MP sergeants who I noticed was wearing plastic gloves, cleared them both and put them in separate paper evidence bags. I knew they were evidence bags as that's what was written on them in big black letters.

'Any other weapons?' he shouted,

I suppose I was looking a bit stunned,

'Yes sir, grenade in my top pocket'

The pin of the grenade was tied into my pocket buttonhole so that by just pulling the grenade out of the pocket the pin would detach, and we would be ready to play. Or not play in this case, this was my get out of jail free card with an instantaneous fuse giving me a quick way out of being captured. The MP must have been familiar with the idea as he sliced the paracord and pulled the grenade free.

'Instant fuse sarge?' he asked, I nodded, and he stripped the fuse out turning the deadly bringer of mayhem back into a paperweight.

He then searched me very quickly and thoroughly, removing my Leatherman, first aid kit and survival kit.

I was standing there still in shock when the CSM spoke to his other sergeant,

'Sergeant MacDuff, handcuff the prisoner.'

He took some shiny metal handcuffs from his belt and we both got a really big shock then as half a dozen rifles were cocked behind me and pointed generally in the direction of the MP's.

Firstly, I was a bit pleased that the guys would be prepared to slot some MP's on my behalf, maybe they didn't hate me as much as I thought they did and secondly, I realised that we were one finger twitch away from a bloodbath.

The CSM must have seen the looks on the guys faces as he went white and stopped talking.

I put my right hand out with the palm down, the combat field signal for slowly or gently, and said loudly.

'No need for handcuffs sergeant-major. I am your prisoner and under your orders. These men have been under my direct command for the entire time, under my direct orders.'

If this was going to rat-shit, then we might as well have just me in the mix rather than the usual military system of blaming all of the junior ranks. As the old saying goes 'The shit that hits the fan will not be evenly distributed'-lol. The paras were looking slightly amused, they weren't going to interfere, so I looked around at Tommo and repeated,

'These men were under my direct orders at all times',

He looked back at me and nodded, great, at least he had got the message and would brief the lads accordingly.

The CSM then made one of the most sensible decisions of his life.

'Forget the handcuffs, Sergeant MacDuff. Prisoner and escort fall in.'

I fell in behind Sgt Mac and the other guy fell in behind me,

I could not resist,

'Lead on MacDuff,'

'Piss off wanker, its "Lay on MacDuff," you tool,'

One-nil to me I think.

'Prisoner and escort, quick march.'

12.

So, our strange little band left the scene of what had been my biggest battle to date and we marched off towards the waiting Chinook which still had its rotors turning. As we approached the aircraft the loadie was waiting for us. He took his right glove off and shook my hand, then he gave me a bottle of water and some ear defenders, they are a brilliant aircraft but they can get a bit noisy inside.

I walked up into the cargo space and found a seat in the middle between the rotors, that being one of the quietest places usually. I was thirsty and was still trying to process what had just happened, so I drank the water in one go.

The big bird lifted off with the usual lurch and then smoothed out as we got airborne. I was starting to calm down and the loadie came back to where I was sitting, this time with a haverbag ration, the military's version of a packed lunch.

The military haverbag ration has two types of sandwich, ham and cheese or cheese and ham, a packet of crisps made by a company you have never heard of, a Mars bar and in this case an orange. The vegetarian option is that you peel the ham off and the vegan option is that you just eat the crisps. (if vegans eat crisps, I'm not sure? I have never knowingly met a vegan but if I do I will ask how Captain Spock is going on.)

I did what every squaddie has done since the dawn of time and ate the Mars bar first, then the crisps, then the sandwich which to be fair was very tasty, just what you need when you have been arrested for war crimes. The story we were we told when I did my recruit training was that haverbag oranges were irradiated to make them last longer and that if you ate one your piss would glow in the dark. (Just like it does when you drink the liquid out of a glow stick when you are drunk, but that's another story). Needless to say, I have never eaten a haverbag orange and was certainly not going to start now.

I got as comfy as I could on the webbing strap seat and as usual on any kind of transport, I fell asleep. I woke up when I felt the engine note change and the aircraft tilted for landing, this was usually when we had to switch on and run out, screaming, rifles at the ready to protect the Chinook as it dropped us off.

No need to rush this time I thought, I assumed we were going back to my base at Bicester, few nights in the cells until the red slime had done the paperwork and then probably be confined to barracks whilst the military justice system, (well not really, there's not much justice in any military system) let's call it the military legal system, ground slowly towards its conclusion.

The loadie was holding us up at the ramp until the pilots came around, they both shook my hand whilst pointedly ignoring the MP's. At least someone was thinking I had done something right then. I walked off the ramp, saw the big painted sign at the side of the helipad announcing our destination and a cold shiver ran down my spine. At least they didn't have the cheek to put 'Welcome' on it, it just said, 'Military Corrective Training Centre, Colchester.' Shit.

So, this was it, not Bicester where I had mates and backup, this was the infamous 'Glasshouse' the military's prison. Someone was taking this whole 'war crimes shit' a bit seriously. There was a Land Rover waiting at the side of the helipad and I got in the back with the ever-cheerful Sgt Mac (not really), still fuck him if he can't take a joke! The other two rode up front with the driver and we drove for about five minutes then entered what looked like a big shed, a roller door closed ominously behind us and we had arrived.

We went into a brightly lit area which looked just like those police station cell blocks you see on the tele, a couple of warrant officers were sitting behind a big desk and I came to attention on the yellow square painted on the floor. The CSM opened the proceedings,

'This is Sgt Michael Lewis, RLC,' (Royal Logistic Corps) which is my home regiment,

'He is under arrest on suspicion of war crimes and murder, he has been cautioned and has made no reply'

Lying shit I thought, I haven't been cautioned at all, however the idea of 'making no reply' was now starting to sound like a good one. The main guy behind the desk was an MP, RSM, (Regimental Sergeant-Major). This is 'The Man' on any army base, the Commanding Officer thinks he runs the base but only because the RSM lets him-lol. He leaned over the desk and shook my hand, not what I was expecting to be honest,

'Sgt Lewis,' he said, 'Damn good job at the siege'.

'Thank you, sir,'

'We will get this shit sorted out and get you settled for tonight',

Well, sounds like I had a least one friend in the camp even if Sgt Mac was chewing on his teeth beside me. A skinny, miserable looking woman with grey hair wearing one of those white paper suits you see on tele came over to me.

'I need to conduct a forensic examination' she said, 'Under Queens Regulations you do not have the right to refuse.'

OK sunshine I thought, time for me to stick to saying nothing.

She indicated a side room just off the main reception area and we went in accompanied by Sgt Mac, if I was going to get a pasting this is where it would happen, out of sight, I tensed up and watched him very carefully, I would probably lose a scrap against an MP but I wasn't going easily and would do some damage to him on the way.

My old Shotokan instructor had taught us some unusual moves, his favourite phrase being,

'OK in the dojo, no good in the chipshop'.

Well I had a range of 'ok in the chipshop' stuff that might work well in the cell block.

But no, Sgt Mac simply stood near the door as if he was just witnessing the proceedings. OK then. Sunshine asked me to take off my jacket, boots, trousers and shirt and put them all in separate paper evidence bags. I did that standing there in just my boxers and socks, it's a good job she's not pretty I thought, or I may well have had an erection to go with my outfit.

She started to swab my right wrist and hand with what looked like a handwipe.

'What's that for?' I asked, breaking my own no-speaking rule,

'Testing for gunshot residue',

'Really, I have just been in a weeklong firefight and you think there may be some gunshot residue on me, fantastic,'.

She didn't find that amusing, so I shut up again and let her get on with it. She didn't take DNA or anything, I suppose because I hadn't been in close contact with any of the enemy apart from Fuckwit the Executioner and it hadn't ended well for him, although to be fair there might be some of his blood spatter still clinging to my trousers.

The thing is I wasn't going to deny what had happened, it had happened, it just depends on whether you look at it as war or not.

She then gave me some orange coveralls with ACM on the back which apparently stands for 'Awaiting Court Martial', to differentiate me from a convicted prisoner.

Sunshine then went back to wherever miserable women live, I did wonder about her sex life, I mean shit, if she can't get laid in a military prison then she is really not trying, still, someone else could have my go, ha ha.

Back into the main room and an older bloke in civvies was waiting for me. He shook my hand,

'Hey up Sarge, I'm Tony if you come with me, we will get you settled,'

Fair enough, I thought. I followed him out and there was another Land-Rover outside,

'Sit in the front mate,' he said.

Better and better I thought, wonder if I can get a brew? I did think a beer was out of the question, but I was gagging for a cup of tea.

We set off and he said,

'We are putting you in the VIP block, keep you away from any prying eyes and any of the inmates who might want a bit of revenge.'

Shit, I hadn't thought about that, of course there would be some prisoners in here with extremist views who might well wish to do me harm, I would need to be on my guard. Bit like being on a training course with guys from a Scottish regiment, great blokes, but they spend most of their leisure time fighting amongst themselves and it's a good idea not to get caught up in the drama.

Two minutes later we pulled up outside a single storey building just marked 'Building 17'. I suppose the idea was to confuse anybody who had broken in, was trying to free the prisoners, and had got past barbed wire, armed guards, savage dogs etc. I had once been on a big military base in the Midlands and had been sent by the guardroom to drop my vehicle off at 'Building 22'. Hours of fruitless searching later I found a young squaddie who pointed at the big (anonymous) building behind me,

'It's that one' he said, as if he was talking to the village idiot.

'Where's the sign then?' I enquired patiently, which is not my usual way of enquiring,

'They sent it off for painting a couple of years ago, but everybody knows its Building 22.'

I had thanked him heartily for his assistance, (not really) and he went on his merry way.

We wandered into the building and it was quite pleasant inside, obviously designed more for officers than plebs like me. Tony took me into what turned out to be the mess room and said,

'Fancy a brew, sarge?'

My hero! A brew was quickly forthcoming as was a packet of crisps and some chocolate digestives-outstanding, this was the best I had felt all day.

We sat down for a chat and it turned out that the enemy had been posting details of the siege on their version of a communications network, this had been seen by anyone who was interested, except us of course, which is why people were shaking my hand and telling me what a good job we had done.

Apparently, the camera that Fuckwit the Executioner had set up to record Isabelle's beheading was still running when I arrived and gave him the good news with his own sword. Naturally half the world wanted me locking up, (guess which half?) and the other half wanted to give me a medal.

'You're stuck in the politics,' Tony said,

'The government are trying to sort out a peace deal with them and you're in the way, which is why you are here.'

Fair enough I thought, I was getting really tired now, tea and choccy biccys were working their magic. I needed to crash somewhere private so I could get the shakes and feel better.

Tony showed me to my cell, which was just like a single room in the mess, shower and toilet, but no tv and no handle inside the door. There was a red button near the door to summon help if I was ill and otherwise, he would see me in the morning.

There were a couple of paperback books on the windowsill, which was handy, but I was too tired even to read and just crashed out on the bed wearing my jumpsuit. I woke up in the middle of the night, took a second to remember where I was and then got the shakes, this had happened to me before but that did not make it any easier. Shit.

13.

There was daylight coming around the curtains in the morning when there was a knock at the door, my watch had been taken and there was no clock, but I assumed it was 7am. Great. I stood to attention as Tony opened the door and came in,

'No need for that Sarge,' he said, 'you are among friends here,'

He handed me an ASDA, All Day Breakfast sandwich, still in its wrapper and a large mug of tea.

'Your lawyers coming at 11, I'll come and get you just before, OK?'

'Yes, fine mate, thanks.'

So, I ate my butty and drank my tea, another fine mess I find myself in, still if the army teaches you anything its patience and if you can't take a joke you shouldn't have joined. I was stuck in this room, but no one was shooting at me, I was being fed and had something to read. I checked the bookshelf out and found that one of them was 'Night Probe' by Clive Cussler, one that I had in my room back at Bicester, always happy to re-read the good stuff.

After about an hour I was bored so I started my daily exercise routine, basic stretches then some tai chi, bit odd you might think for a soldier but I had served on a base near Grantham where we actually had a tai chi club which is where I picked up the interest. I wasn't really athletic enough for competitive team sports, especially the way the military played them, although I did run to keep fit and enjoyed rock climbing when I got the chance. Both those interests looked like being a bit thin on the ground now, but I could do the tai chi anywhere.

Soon enough Tony knocked at the door again and we were off to an interview room where there was a frazzled looking major from the Army Legal Service, sitting at a desk. He stunk of cigarettes and did not look happy.

'I have spoken to the Judge Advocate, and he has agreed that if you plead guilty, he will not consider the death penalty'

'Death penalty?'

'Yes, you can be executed by firing squad for war crimes. They are saying that you killed seven hundred and eighty-one people in that engagement including eleven women and children.'

Fuck me, this had just got a bit serious,

'So, what then lock me up for life?'

'Yes, the War Crimes Tribunal in the Hague are screaming for you to be sent there but at the moment we have primacy, so we need to get you sentenced quickly before they go to the International Criminal Court to have you extradited. We will plead guilty, the Court Martial is on Wednesday and then you will serve your sentence here.'

'All sorted then?'

'Yes, the Army wants this done and so does the government, then the peace talks can proceed.'

Ah well, seems like I'm the statue in this little scenario, (you know the saying, 'some days you're the pigeon and some days you're the statue,' lol.)

'So, what's next then sir?'

He handed me a sheet of paper,

'Sign this, the doctor will see you this afternoon and she will find you fit to be court-martialled, then I will see you on Wednesday.'

'Very good sir.'

I signed, because it all seemed to be cut and dried so I might as well just go along with it, another thing the army teaches you. No worries.

Then back to the room, I can't really call it a cell even though it was, another brew and an ASDA Ploughman's Lunch sandwich, a Kit Kat, and a banana. Tasty.

Then first thing in the afternoon it was back to the interview room to see the Doctor, a Medical Corps Colonel, who was apparently a psychiatrist. (My first time with one of those.)

Tony closed the door as he went out and she began her examination.

'Are you some kind of fucking maniac?'

'You tell me,' I said, 'you're the fucking shrink'

'Don't speak to me like that, I'll put you on a charge for insubordination,'

'Join the fucking queue, Colonel, right now, you are the least of my worries.'

You might have noticed that I had formally 'lost the plot' at this point, I never react well to aggression from anyone, a hangover from my shitty childhood.

'You have murdered innocent civilians, you maniac,'

'Bollocks ma'am they were shooting at me,'

She was almost flying with rage at this point, I had chosen an imaginary line on the table and if she came over that I was going to smack her, woman, colonel, doctor or whatever, my shit taking days were now officially over.

'No, they weren't, you fuckwit, you bombed their houses killing women and children, the younger ones came at you the following day because they were scared of more attacks and you blitzed them. They sent one of their leaders, with a white flag, a white fucking flag, you moron, and you killed him and then destroyed the ambulance they sent to pick him up.

They were defending themselves, the sniper in the tower was a lone gunman and you destroyed their town hall, all they wanted you to do was stop bombing them. They had to keep attacking you to hold you back, the performance with Isabelle was just that, they were trying to get you to talk to them they weren't going to kill her, just get your attention and then you did your 'Mission Impossible' act and killed even more of them.

The meeting in the church was to talk about how they could stop the fighting, they were all going to leave their homes and get out of your way, you blew the church to shit and then dropped white phosphorus on them. You absolute fucking animal.'

'Fuck you Colonel, and fuck the horse you rode in on, if you believe all that shit then we have nothing more to say. All they had to do was stop and leave us alone'

I literally thought she would explode, she had gone bright red and I wondered if she was having a heart attack, good luck getting any first aid from me I thought, I would just sit there and watch the bitch die. I stood up and went to the door,

'This examination is not over,'

'Yes, it is colonel, you left wing, namby-pamby, commie-loving, pinko-shagging pathetic excuse for a soldier.'

Wow, I had even surprised myself with that lot, perhaps her therapeutic intervention had worked, and I was now getting in touch with my inner peaceful spirit. Yes, I did once have a girlfriend who was doing psychology at college I must have absorbed more of the psychobabble from her than I thought.

Surprising because she always said I didn't listen, at least I think that's what she said. (never gets old that one).

I opened the door and walked out into the corridor, Tony was standing there looking a bit shaken, I realised that he must have heard the exchange from outside.

'All sorted mate, apparently it's a new technique specially for helping war criminals, can we go back for a brew now please?'

That was Sunday sorted, I wasn't stressed about the colonel. Not sure how she would be able to explain what had happened to her bosses and as I was facing a considerable time in the army's worst jail I didn't think she could do much to me anyway.

14.

Monday came around and I got my first taste of exercise, there is a small enclosed courtyard in the middle of the block about ten metres by five. Tony was off so Dave, a retired EOD technician, (EOD is basically the bomb squad) escorted me to the yard. EOD's are great guys but they are all deaf from all the explosives, so with a bit of shouting and hand signals I checked that I could run if I wished and had an hour's slot. Great, I had done my tai chi that morning and this was my first taste of fresh air since last week. I started jogging around, warmed up then worked out a routine of going steady down the long side and sprinting down the short side. Not ideal but I was making the best of it.

I warmed down when we back to the room and had a shower. Feeling better now than I had since before the siege so that was good.

Tea was an ASDA chicken triple sandwich, a Twix and a banana, very nice. I settled down for the evening with my book, expecting to go for a tea and toast with the lads at about nine o'clock. However, a bit earlier than that Dave knocked and came into the room.

'You have a visitor',

This was a surprise, perhaps Lisa had come in for a conjugal visit or Isabelle had sneaked in to say thanks for saving her life with a quick hand-job. Not really, it would probably be some boring army clerical matter, some company clerk querying a mileage claim I had made six months ago or chasing up my latest mess bill!

I followed Dave to what was identified on the door as the Training Room, Dave opened the door, leaned in and said,

'Sgt Lewis, sir.'

Ok, I went in and saw a young, fit looking bloke, standing looking out of the window. I didn't know who he was, but I knew what he was, this guy was Special Forces.

I had worked with them a few times in some dim and distant parts of the world and they all had the same look. A mixture of energy, danger and confidence I suppose.

They would often show up in the middle of the night needing a new vehicle or some old, shot-to-shit wreck fixing, we would sort them out and they would disappear into the gloom. The good thing for us was that there was never any paperwork, we just had a code to set against any stores that we used. This meant that after a 'visit' from them we could sort out all of the shortfall in our inventory, code it to the SF team and no one would ever be able to check – result.

'Michael, good to see you, Colin Warner from the Regiment.'

He walked across to me and shook my hand,

'Evening sir,'

Shit I thought, SAS, I had finally hit the big time. He pointed to the table in the middle of the room and I saw a McDonalds take-out bag which smelt amazing, and a six pack of cold looking Stella Artois. This man had now become my new best friend.

'Help yourself, wondered if we could have a chat about the siege, completely off the record of course, we always try and learn lessons from combat engagements, so I wanted to pick your brains if that's ok?'

Well it was ok with me, and as I was halfway through the first can of Stella I just nodded, finished the can and sat down. That one didn't touch the sides as they say so I opened another, took a deep swig and said,

'Yes, sir, no problem'.

'Help yourself to a burger when you are ready,'

I rooted around in the bag and found a big mac, a quarterpounder and a veggie burger. No fries and no milkshake, still you can't have everything.

''What do you need to know sir?'

'I'll start from the beginning if that's OK, when you took over the unit you had fourteen guys is that right,

I nodded, didn't want to speak with a mouthful of big mac.

'When you first ordered them to bomb the village you had to threaten Corporal Thompson with your rifle, would you have shot him if he had refused?'

I thought about it,

'No, I don't think so, I was desperately scared at that point, I felt very responsible for those guys, I needed to get us to safety. I suppose at one level I thought that Tommo could put the blame on me if the shit hit the fan but also at that stage I wasn't expecting to survive.'

'OK then, next you shot the chap with the white flag and blew up the ambulance?'

'Thought they were suicide bombers.' I said opening the third can.

'Fair enough, what made you go down the rope to get the paramedic instead of just shooting her?'

I smiled,

'The look in her eyes'

He looked at me.

'I saw her through the gunsight, if she had looked scared I would have shot her straight away, but she didn't look scared, she looked angry. She was pissed off at the way she was being treated, she was showing some amazing spirit in the circumstances so I thought it was worth a chance at grabbing her. Anyway, she has a great arse.'

'Before you went down to get her you shot the militant who was holding her and then you executed him with his own sword.'

'Yes, lucky shot I suppose, he was just winded and I had left my weapon up top, so just I used what was handy.'

'Not really,' he said and reached down into a black sports bag by his feet. He pulled out a ceramic, body armour chest plate that had corner to corner red lines drawn on. In the dead centre, where the lines crossed was a bullet impact mark.

'We recovered a lot of stuff from the scene and when I saw this I was curious. There are six lanes on our thousand-yard range at Hereford, so I got the rangemaster to set up six dummies with body armour at five hundred and forty-two metres, that was the range you shot him at.'

Didn't know where he was going with this so I said nothing, finished the third can and started on the quarterpounder.

'I took six rifles from the armoury, then went to 'A' squadrons barracks and asked for six volunteers who were not sniper trained. I let them have five sighting shots on a separate target and then one shot each at the chest plate on the dummies. They all hit it of course, they would have been in trouble if they hadn't, but none of them hit it dead centre as you had.'

'I'm sorry sir, but what's your point?' Listen to me, three cans in and talking back to an officer – lol!

'My point is that you deliberately hit the centre of his chest plate so that he would still be alive when you arrived, giving you the opportunity to behead him.

I have checked your marksmanship history sergeant you can shoot. So it was not just a lucky shot'

I smiled, busted.   I nodded.

'I have seen a number of beheading videos as I am sure that you have sir, I just wanted them to see what it felt like.'

'So you knew about the camera?'

'Yes, didn't know it was still working but I was hoping it was.'

'Outstanding.'

High praise indeed from this guy.

'Going back for a minute, what about the sniper then, why did you risk yourself, you were in command you could have ordered one of the troopers to run the gauntlet?'

That question was so ridiculous I didn't even bother to answer him, just opened the fourth can.

He waited a second or two then nodded,

'Moving on, what can you tell me about the library, I understand the women there had set up an informal brothel?'

'I have no knowledge of any such arrangement, sir.'

I was four cans in now and I had eaten two of his burgers so there was nothing much left for him to tempt me with, plus I was getting a bit pissed, two cans was usually my limit these days, and over a much longer period of time.

'And what happened with trooper Morgan?'

'A fine upstanding trooper sir, a credit to his unit, bit tricky to understand when he gets excited but I think that's a Geordie thing anyway.'

I wasn't exactly slurring my words but I wasn't far off. No way was I going to grass trooper Morgan up, or the 'ladies of the library.' I was sure Tommo had given the lads the 'official' story and they would be sticking to it. I had been grassed up myself a couple of times and I hated it.

'Fine, I just wanted to let you know that what you did at the siege affected the whole outcome of the conflict, they were so outraged that you had bombed the church that they pulled fighters from all over the area to wipe you out. That let us roll up the smaller units and get you some help.'

'Thank you sir.'

'One last thing, did you really fix bayonets?'

'Yes, we were going to go down fighting,'

'Outstanding, I have been in fourteen years and have never given that order,'

There was a pause so I opened another can.

'Just to recap sarge, I was never here, this never happened, and you need to finish that fifth can before I go, I need to take all the evidence with me.'

'Thank you very much sir, might be the last beer I have for a while.'

'You're welcome, good luck on Wednesday.'

'No worries, they are looking after me very well here and if I get a long sentence then so be it.'

'Not angry about being scapegoated?'

'What would be the point?

'Fair enough,'

He yelled out to Dave that we were finished, with no effect,

'He's a bit deaf sir, ex-EOD'

He smiled, I got up and carefully made my way to the door, wow five cans of Stella in about forty minutes, I was bladdered.

Wednesday rolled around as I knew it would and I was taken to the court-martial building for my appearance. Lots of people wandering about studiously ignoring me as if I were invisible, fine by me.

I was escorted into the courtroom and sat down at a small table next to my ciggy-smelling lawyer who looked even more anxious than I was. We all stood up and the panel of three officers walked in. The guys had said there could be up to seven of them but I got two colonels and a brigadier general who was the judge, fair enough.

We sat down and the judge started giving the history of the case, to be fair I zoned out a bit then. I had always been in lots of trouble at home and at school and when people were shouting at me I just switched off and went to a happy place in my head. My lawyer was talking and then he nudged me and we stood up again.

The judge then spoke,

'Sgt Michael Lewis, you have pleaded guilty to the grave offences of war crimes and murder of non-combatants in a military engagement. You are hereby dishonourably discharged from the British Army and sentenced to forty-five years imprisonment to be served at the military corrective training centre. Then you will be handed over to the jurisdiction of the War Crimes Tribunal for any action they wish to take. Do you have anything to say?'

'Yes sir,'

I had been told not to speak but hey-ho what were they going to do to me now?

My lawyer put his hand on my arm but I shrugged him off, the judge glared at him but this was my one chance when they had to listen to me, it was in the rules.

'When I arrived at the police station I had fourteen troops under my command and there were forty-two women and children needing our protection. Five days later when we were relieved by the Parachute Regiment I still had fourteen troops and forty-two women and children safe and well in the building. I did my job sir protecting my soldiers and the civilians. Just making the point sir.'

'Have you finished?'

Well yes General I have, I did think of adding, 'and fuck you if you can't take a joke' but the joke seemed to be on me today, shit, forty-five years, I would be seventy three when I got out, that's a fucking shedload of ASDA sandwiches.

The panel stood up and left.

'That was stupid,' my lawyer said,

'Why sir, do you think I might be in some sort of trouble?' I laughed.

He said nothing, the escort guys took me out and back to the block where I was issued with a different pair of orange overalls this time with CP on the back, standing for convicted prisoner, great.

The good news after this was that they kept me in the special unit, they claimed that I would be at risk of reprisals if I went into the main prisoner population but it was really that the covert systems that operate in the military were looking after me. So I still had my own room, exercise every day and a resupply of library books whenever I wanted.

I also had a visit from a rather pretty Education Corps captain who said that I was now eligible to undertake Open University courses at the army's expense. She left me a handbook and whilst it was too soon for me to get my head round that for now, I did work out that if I really tried hard then I could have fifteen university degrees when I left the centre, do you think that would enhance my career prospects as the brochure seemed to be implying-lol?

15.

They had escorted me to the mess room as they usually did about 9pm to have tea and toast, talk about football and for me to make my flask for the night; Tony who was the shift supervisor, pointed back towards my room and said.

'You go on Sarge; I will be along in a minute.'

He still insisted on using my old rank even though my dishonourable discharge meant that it no longer applied.

This was really unusual, but things had calmed down a lot since my court martial and I guess they were just being more relaxed with me. I turned the corridor leading to my room and saw Colin Warner standing outside it.

'Want to come and work for me?' He said.

'Yes please'

He set off down the corridor past my room and went out through the fire exit. I followed him and saw a dark blue Jaguar parked in the alley behind the building. He flicked the boot release and I saw blankets and pillows inside along with bags of crisps and bottles of water.

'Dive in' he said, ' long way to go',

I did not need asking twice, what did I have to lose, they could have shot me anytime, 'attempting to escape' and I did not think they would involve outsiders like SF in that type of situation?

I climbed into the boot and we set off, I felt the car slow for the exit gate, and heard a muffled conversation.

'Can you open the boot sir?' The guard asked.

There was a short reply involving a suggestion as to what the guard could do with his request and then we drove off, boot safely unopened.

I was too wired to sleep but I did start dozing even though I was desperately wondering what was happening.

After about two hours the car slowed and stopped, the boot opened and I climbed out, we were up a track in a dark wood with only the car sidelights to see by. I was really stiff and stumbled to the side of the road.

'Piss break' he said, 'we are about halfway'

Fair enough, I did, climbed into the boot again and off we went.

I dozed off again, it was fairly comfortable in the boot if a little cramped. Eventually I felt the car slowing and stopping, again with the muffled conversation, the noise of a gate rolling back and then we were moving.

We stopped and the boot popped open, I climbed wearily out and stood blinking in the harsh halogen streetlights of the camp. We were parked on a slight hill next to a single storey building with the very welcome sign outside saying, '22 SAS - WO and Sgt's Mess.' Shit I had really hit the jackpot.

'They are expecting you - from now on you are Sgt D.A. Smith '

'What's D.A. for?'

'Don't Ask - lets people know not to pry - just call yourself Michael, let your hair and beard grow - that will help you blend in; boss wants to see you at ten tomorrow and then fourteen hundred at the vehicle sheds ready for work'

Could this crazy night get any better I thought? Not much time to acclimatise - you usually get a couple of days grace on a new posting but considering the alternative I was ready to start work now so a night's sleep would be a bonus.

I walked into the entrance hall, very conscious of my bright orange overalls and saw a young woman walk out from behind the reception desk. She was about twenty-two with long dark hair and gorgeous brown eyes, very attractive - another bonus.

'Sgt Smith, we have been expecting you, welcome, my name is Laura I am one of the deputy mess managers'

'Thank you - it's nice to meet you'

I know sparkling repartee as usual, I was not good with women, I had been a very anxious teenager and that does not play well with teenage girls, I had experienced a few relationships with adult women but the military and my lack of skills always seemed to get in the way of them.

'You are in room fourteen, turn right at the end of the corridor, it's the last room on the left'

She handed me a yale type key with a brass disc on a ring with the number fourteen on.

'There is food in the dining room and the chefs start at 5 so please don't go hungry'

I realised that I was still clutching my night flask from my last accommodation so did not think I would be too stressed before breakfast.

I took the key and walked off to find my room.

I had gone a few paces when Laura said.

'Sgt Smith, some of us lost people in the wars - thank you for what you did'

So much for 'Don't ask' - still if they can't keep secrets here then we are all stuffed.

'You're welcome'

Again, great repartee dickhead, I had been involved in the death of 781 people in what now seemed to be one of the most crucial actions of the conflict and the best I could do was 'You're welcome', Ah well it was late.

I reached my room and opened the door and stood there amazed, this was my room. No, not just my room, this was 'My Room' from Bicester. They must have recovered all of my possessions after the court martial and relocated them here. My guitar, tele, various pictures and souvenirs, I checked the wardrobe and found my uniform and civvies hanging neatly in rows.

I checked the uniforms and saw that my name badges had been replaced with 'Smith D. A.' but the badges had been aged to match my well washed and faded uniforms. My fridge contained beer, cheese and fresh milk and my drinks tray included an unopened bottle of Southern Comfort replacing the half empty one I had left in Bicester – wow, talk about attention to detail - I was impressed.

There was a small brown envelope on the drinks tray on my chest of drawers, it had, 'Naafi money' written on it in pencil. I looked inside and saw five twenty-pound notes, I was a bit puzzled by this but then I realised that as a convicted prisoner I had no pay and so no income.

I remembered signing some forms at the CTC donating the entire contents of my bank accounts and all my worldly goods to a military charity, so at least now I would be able to replenish my drinks and snacks when I needed to. They really had thought of everything. I was very grateful.

I was also exhausted, there was ice in the fridge so with a healthy slug of my favourite bourbon I stretched out on the bed and went to sleep.

I was awake early; the sounds of activity that are present in all military accommodation started about five-thirty. I dozed for a while then realised I was hungry, I had a quick shower, which included new supplies of my favourite shampoo and soaps, slipped into my 'working dress' of green denim uniform and wandered out to find some food.

I had put my uniform on as I was not sure what the dress code was, some messes allow track suits at breakfast and some don't.

I reached the main restaurant area and realised that there was no dress code. It was like the Cantina scene from Star Wars, men of all races and sizes, and even a few women, in all stages of dress and undress, one guy was just wearing shorts and nothing else, he had a range of what looked like shrapnel injuries on his back so I wondered if that was just part of the healing process. No worries about the dress code then, easier for me to blend in I thought. I was mistaken.

One of the guys caught sight of me and stood up, others noticed and also stood up, staring at me, the room fell silent and then they started applauding - shit. I just nodded and smiled saying 'Thank you' over and over again and then walked to the hotplate for some nosh.

At least that saved on introductions, I would hope to keep a low profile in the future, but I was starting to see that not everyone thought that my actions at the siege had been a bad thing. I needed to remember that the people in this camp were warriors and warriors fight, that's what they do.

I later found out that SAS troopers scored themselves informally on the number of kills they had made so with allegedly seven hundred and eighty-one kills to my name, I was in the lead by some considerable distance.

Food was great, usual army standard, the difference here was that there was no knobhead cook's assistant saying 'just one sausage' as they usually did.

I joined one of the tables and was relieved when after a few nods of greeting everyone else got on with their breakfast. Hunger satisfied I went back to my room collecting a paper from the stand in the hallway. I had not seen the news for several weeks and was pleased to read that it was the usual drivel about nothing and that my 'escape' had not made the front page, or any other page for that matter.

I suppose if you went to the trouble of renewing someone's shower products and ageing their uniform name tapes then you could probably cover up a missing war criminal.

16.

Later that morning I made my way over to the HQ admin building. I arrived at 9.45 because that's what 10am is in army speak. I found the Commanding Officers office fairly easily, it had 'Commanding Officer' written on the door, his admin staff was a young male captain who seemed reasonably pleased to see me. I took a chair and waited. The place was buzzing as I expected it would be most days.

'Colonel Anstey will see you now, sergeant.'

'Thank you, sir.'

I marched in and came to attention in front of his desk. I had never heard of this guy but apparently, he was highly regarded by the troops which is good. He welcomed me to the base and told me to see Major Warner if there were any problems. Standard C.O. welcome really although one thing puzzled me that I was only able to work out afterwards. He was known as 'Paddy' but the guy I met had a broad Yorkshire accent, he would make Jeremy Clarkson sound like a cockney.

Turns out that his full name was Ian Reginald Anstey and he had arrived at Sandhurst on his first day with his initials on his briefcase. His briefcase was blown up by the training staff later that day and he had been 'Paddy' ever since.

Standard two minute 'Hello and welcome' no worries, heard that a million times, so back out of the office and the captain said.

'RSM would like to see you next sarge then you can shoot off.'

Very good, as I have mentioned the RSM is the powerhouse on any military base, usually very experienced, strict but fair. I would imagine in a place like this that he would be a bit special, well I was partially right because he turned out to be a bit 'special needs.'

'You are a fucking baby killer,' he screamed into my face as soon as the office door was closed.

He was a little man, a scouser which was a bit of a disappointment for me as all of the scousers I had worked with were great blokes, comedians to a man, they took a while to get to know you but once they did you were mates for life. To have this arsehole yelling at me without even a hello was a bit much.

He was not alone; a big ugly sergeant was standing at the side of the desk smirking.

'You should be in a prison cell blah de blah de blah,'

Yes, by this point I had tuned out, I had met people like this before, they are all over the military unfortunately, but I had expected that the staff in this regiment would be a bit more professional.

There was a bit of a silence and I tuned back in.

'I said, do you understand me?'

I did think of saying that I did not understand, in my best French but funny replies would have been wasted on this cretin, so I shouted. 'Yes sir.'

'Get the fuck out of my office,'

'Yes sir.'

I found out afterwards that he was not highly regarded on the base, he was known as the, 'Poison Dwarf' or PD for short, he had been a favourite of the previous CO which is how he had got the job and his mate was known as 'Shrek,' for obvious reasons although not to his face. Unless you were a 'blade', one of the badged members of the regiment, and they called him whatever the fuck they wanted.

Despite his looks and size, he was known as a 'milk carton', because he had 'no bottle'.

Fairly typical morning when you arrive at a new posting, I did want to have a look around the camp but I thought I had better not just wander about willy-nilly, so I went back to the mess and enjoyed my lunch. (ASDA sandwiches are great but not for every meal-lol)

One-thirty pm, I asked directions to the vehicle sheds and went to meet the team. This was my natural environment, vehicles, tools, camaraderie, interesting work with good people. I am not a mortar man and not really a combat leader so to be 'back where I belong' felt great.

The boss was a CSM, named Dougie. He was a softly spoken Brummie and he put the kettle on straight away. Being in my own trade we chatted about where we had served, who we knew and where our careers might have crossed in the past.

We finished our brew and he introduced me to the rest of the team, there were two privates and two corporals, they were all pleased to see me because apart from anything else I would be an extra pair of hands in the workshop. Their workload was based around five guys so I would hopefully be a useful addition, another point in my favour is that I am a biker, a motorcycle fan, surprisingly the only one on the team. Guess who would be sorting all the bikes out from here on in?

'Do you play football?'

'Not very well.'

'Great, you can be the goalie then.'

Fair enough, I had been co-opted into many different sports teams in my time and just as quickly co-opted out of them when they realised how crap I was. The situation here is that the guys liked to play in the camp five-a-side league and were doing quite well as every time one of the squadrons got a good team going some or all of them would be sent off on operations.

It suited me, indoors, wearing a tracksuit, and not having close physical contact sounded good I just had one worry.

'Isn't it a bit dangerous playing against the SAS lads?'

I would not play against paras, or guys from a Scottish regiment for example. My teeth and my bollocks are far too important to me.

Dougie explained that whilst they had a fearsome reputation, they were also incredibly disciplined and however much 'verbal' there was or however 'clumsy' the tackling was they never ever reacted. He mentioned that there had been one occasion years ago when a 'blade' had got so fed up with endless clumsy tackles from a player in the cookhouse team that he had grabbed his shirt and shouted at him. The blade was out of the regiment and off the base the same day.

The SAS vehicle section was a plum posting for anyone in my trade, Dougie explained that in addition to the usual army stuff we all knew about, on this base we got to play with all manner of weird and wonderful stuff that the manufacturers had sent for testing or that the regiment wanted to try out. Brilliant.

He then led me to a massive Snap-On toolkit sitting just outside his office,

'Ta-da,'

He said, I must have looked puzzled,

'Your new toolkit,'

'No way,'

Yes, we have all got one, it's a bonus of working here, whatever you want, whenever you want it just let me know.'

'Won't it get nicked?'

'Not on this base mate, whatever they want they get so why would they nick yours? You could leave your wallet on the desk and it wouldn't get touched unless they put some gay porn in it.'

Well that had happened to me before, so I was careful with my wallet, that reminds me I will have to buy one from the Naafi.

I stayed chatting and wandering about the sheds for the rest of the afternoon and then started into a normal working routine. 7.30 start, brew at 10, lunch at 12.30 brew at 2.30 and finish usually about 4 unless it was Wednesday when we finished at lunchtime and played footy in the afternoon. Saturday could be a half day or longer and Sunday was usually a day off. Great. If there was a big job on we all chipped in and worked until it was finished.

17.

One Friday evening I was sitting in my room reading, it had been a busy week and I was tired, when there was a knock at the door. I opened it and there was Laura looking amazing in trousers and a soft wool jumper.

'Can I speak to you?'

'Certainly, do you want to come in or speak outside?

'I will come in please it's a bit personal.'

OK, I went back into the room and sat on the bed so that she could sit in my armchair.

'My husband was a trooper in B squadron, he was killed in the civil war,'

'I'm sorry,'

We had lost a couple of hundred British troops in the conflict, the enemy having proved to be a well-armed and very determined bunch.

'The thing is,' she paused, 'He always promised me that he would freeze his sperm so that if anything happened to him, I could still have his baby.'

She paused again.

'He never did so I have come to ask if you would make me pregnant? I want my baby's daddy to be a warrior and with your record I can at least think that the people who killed Steven got some payback.'

Whoa!, Stop, Handbrake on! WTF?

I said nothing, what could I say? All of the women I had ever had sex with had been very insistent on me not making them pregnant, so I was a bit off-piste with this one.

'You wouldn't have to look after the baby, I want to leave Hereford and go back home. My dad has a car dealership in Northumberland, I was working there when I met Steve. They live in a big house in the countryside and my mum would go bonkers to have a grandchild. It would mean that I could go back home, tell everyone that it is Steve's baby and get on with the rest of my life, I would have something positive out of this tragedy.'

Wow.

I'm not going to come in a plastic cup,' I said, having thought things through a little.

'I would want to have proper sex with you.' I said.

Yes dickhead, proper sex you moron, she's not going to get pregnant from a blow job is she? Come on, this is all a bit new for me.

'Yes, that's fine I would have more chance of conceiving that way'

OK then.

'Have you got a plan?'

Nice chat up line Romeo.

'Yes, can I tell you?'

'Yes.'

'I am ovulating this weekend starting today, if we put a pillow under my bum and you lift my legs in the air and do it and then when you have finished if you turn around and let me rest my legs on your back for ten minutes then it gives it chance to go all of the way up into me.'

Wow again.

'Is that OK?' she said.

'Yes, that's fine,'

I walked over and locked the door. When I turned around she had put a pillow on the bed and was lying on it. I moved onto the bed and knelt between her open legs.

'How do you want to do this?'

She lifted her legs in the air resting her feet either side of my head. Then she undid her trousers and pulled them and her panties down to the tops of her thighs.

'Can you manage there?'

'Yes.'

I undid my trousers and boxers and snuggled up to where she was. I looked around for a condom and then thought, Doh!

I moved in closer to her and slipped a couple of fingers in her pussy by way of foreplay. Her eyes were closed, and I slipped my dick into her, feeling a bit of resistance but she was young enough to have a nice wet pussy anyway. A few strokes and it was all over, in my defence she is very gorgeous and she did want me to come rather than for her to enjoy the shag, so I was doing her a favour really. Really.

I waited a few minutes and then she asked me to turn around, I did and she wriggled into her clothes and rested her legs on my back.

I literally could not think of anything to say.

After a couple of minutes, she spoke,

'Was that OK for you?'

Well yes it was actually, my first ever bareback ride, I wasn't really conscious of the difference, but it was great sex with a beautiful woman, what's not to like?

'Yes, it was amazing.'

I told you I was smooth didn't I? To be honest I was a bit shocked, it was about five minutes since she knocked on my door and now she might be carrying my baby.

'It's ok now you can move, thanks,'

I slid off the bed and she stood up.

'Will it be ok to come back tomorrow?'

Bless her, she looked so serious that all of the stupid comments I could have made stayed in my head and I just said,

'Yes sure.'

'Will you promise not to tell anyone?'

'Yes, but think about it Laura you are so gorgeous, if I did tell anyone they would never believe me.'

She smiled at that.

I opened the door slowly and as the corridor was clear she slipped out and away, not even a kiss. I tried to read my book again, but it was no good, I just sat there grinning and drinking for the rest of the night. Wow.

The next day was Saturday and we worked all day sorting some BV 206's for the arctic warfare training (it's like a Snow-Cat) that was planned for next week. I loved these because they have a big Merc engine and they can swim on their tracks.

I was in my room showered, shaved, and wearing my best aftershave, actually my only aftershave and at just before eight there was a gentle tap on the door. Hoping that it was Laura and not the RSM (joke). I opened it and luckily it was Laura.

I was less off balance tonight and I took her in my arms and tried to kiss her. She moved her head away and I kissed her cheek. She tried to move towards the bed, but I held her with her back against the door and my face very close to hers. I looked at her for a couple of seconds and then kissed her again, she got the message and let me kiss her properly. Amazing.

'Hey,' she said.

'Hey nothing'. I said and kissed her again.

She realised that she was at a bit of a disadvantage now, she wanted a dose of Michael's magic baby juice and she was going to have to kiss this frog if she wanted to give birth to a prince in nine months' time. Yes, I know its rubbish but give me a break, the number of beautiful young women who have asked me to have sex with them could be counted on the fingers of one finger. I remember the old joke that says,

'I have never been to bed with an ugly woman, but I have sure woken up with a few'.

It's a bit unkind but you know what I mean.

'I haven't got long' she said.

Well you have come to the right place then, I thought, 'Super sperm in seconds', could be my advertising slogan, 'Tell all of your friends', maybe not.

I let her go then and she moved over to the bed, moved the pillow to the middle and climbed onto it, she held her legs in the air until I got close enough for her to rest them on my shoulders again.

We adjusted our clothing and with a little careful finger play I entered her, wow. This time I was able to enjoy the bareback ride and as I had come last night I was going to take a lot longer this evening to achieve the desired result.

I leaned forward pushing her legs back towards her tits, she was very supple, I reached out and grabbed her wrists and pushed them down on the bed either side of her head. She was now trapped on the end of my dick. I leaned down to kiss her, and she turned away again so I stopped thrusting and waited. She didn't really have a choice and she turned her head back towards me and accepted my kiss, I started thrusting again and we were both happy. I varied the speed and frequency of my thrusting sometimes pulling it almost out before slamming it back in.

She was moaning now, and I was hoping that it was in pleasure not discomfort. I don't have a big dick, (trust me when you shower with hundreds of blokes you soon know that you don't have a big dick) so I don't think I was hurting her.

Then I came, and I held her very close for a few seconds before I let her go, eased out of her, and swivelled around on the bed. She was breathing heavily, more so than last night so I must have been doing something right.

We didn't speak, and after a few minutes she tapped my shoulder and I eased off the bed. I went to stand by the door and waited for her, she had two red spots on her cheeks which I was hoping were passion rather than anger but hey-ho I had enjoyed myself and she had received another delivery of the Jubilee Jism, (I know, I know, I am running out of different words for spunk).

I checked the corridor and then she was gone. Not sure that she will be coming back, maybe I had been a bit too assertive but to be fair it was a transaction and I had really enjoyed my part.

Sunday was great as usual, leisurely brunch. Then a walk, then the Formula One on the tele followed by another nice meal. I showered and shaved just in case and I was surprised when there was a soft tap on the door just before eight. Laura or the poison dwarf I thought, not really. It was Laura.

I held the door open with my hand so that she had to step into my arms, she did that and I kissed her, on the lips. I undid her trousers and pulled them down past her hips, she didn't argue, I thought I would chance it and slipped my hand up to her breast. She didn't stop me, so I pulled her jumper up over her head and saw her bra, great. It was white and lacy and matched her knickers, almost as if she expected to be getting her kit off I thought.

I held her and kissed for a few minutes and then I gently tried to put my tongue in her mouth, this was usually a sticking point for some of the very fussy women I had romanced over the years. But not this time, she opened her lips a fraction and we enjoyed some tongue tickling action for a couple of minutes until we came up for air. Wow this was going well.

I reached behind her and carefully with two hands undid her bra, I pulled it free of her body and she put her arms up to cover her nipples. This let me run my fingers down her sides collecting her knickers and her trousers in the same move. She stepped out of them and then she was naked.

I pulled my shirt over my head and dropped my tracksuit bottoms, (easy on easy off) to the floor. We were both naked now and I held her very tight with my cock up against her stomach and my tongue in her mouth.

After a couple of minutes, I led her to the bed where the pillow was waiting for her arse. She lay back on the bed but instead of jumping straight in, I lay down beside her and began to kiss and caress her with my hands. When I reached her pussy, it was really wet, and she started moaning and this time I am pretty sure it was pleasure. I put her hand on my cock and she started stroking me.

I couldn't trust myself not to come in her mouth, so I just rolled onto her and slipped it in. It was great, she was so relaxed that we just moved together for what seemed like ages before I came and she held me really, really tightly.

I don't know much, anything really, about getting women pregnant, but I was pretty sure that her eggs would not be hot for many more days and that this might be the last time that I enjoyed this fabulous young woman. I held her for a long time until she said.

'You have to let me go sometime.'

'I know, just wanted to remember the moment.'

I said I was smooth didn't I, just sowing the seeds for next month if this weekend's delivery did not do the trick. So off she went, hopefully with child or maybe not because I had some great ideas if she needed servicing next month, involving black lacy underwear, stockings, and suspenders, I know, I know, what was she going to wear-lol!

But it was not to be, I saw her occasionally around the mess and then she was gone, the magic baby juice having done its work. Not sure how I felt about being a sperm donor and having a child I would never see but to be fair this was more than I had ever imagined for myself, so I suppose I was happy with the result. Thinking about it she had no reason to tell anyone about me and every reason not to, so there was very little chance of little Steve or Stephanie coming to find me in eighteen years' time.

18.

I settled back into the routine on the camp, this was one of the best postings I had ever had, really good atmosphere in the sheds, staying out of the RSM's way, not difficult because he never came to the sheds and enjoying keeping myself fit and playing footy. I turned out to have a natural talent as a five-a-side goalkeeper. I stand in one place and the ball bounces off me, I can handle that.

One aspect of my military skills was improving no end. I had been a shit shot with a pistol until I arrived on the SAS base. One evening I had been out for a run when I went past the armoury and saw Charlie, the armourer gazing at a pile of boxes.

It turned out that he had just had a delivery of fifty brand new Heckler and Koch rifles that had to be unpacked, degreased, and prepped for issue the following day. Naturally, I offered to help, and we ended up doing half each and drinking lots of tea during the process. I then had a friend for life and Charlie was happy for me to sign out any weapons I wanted to play with and as much ammo as I could carry.

I then spent many evenings on the indoor twenty-five metre pistol range, not improving very much until the rangemaster took pity on me and taught me how to shoot. Since then I had fired hundreds of rounds each week through a variety of handguns. I am still struggling with the double tap though as my second shot tended to go wide.

I was having a brew with Charlie one Saturday afternoon when he pointed to a stack of big plastic carrying cases in the corner of his workshop, I thought he wanted help with them but no.

'How would you like a go with one of those?'

I opened the box and found a massive Barrett sniper rifle with an amazing telescopic sight.

'Would they let me?'

I'm not sniper trained and have no need to practice with this massive cannon.

'Yes, just tell them you are test firing it for me, I am supposed to test all of these weapons but there is no way that I have time so if you want to take one out onto the thousand-yard range you would be doing me a favour.'

Outstanding.

I borrowed his golf cart and made my way to the range with the big Barrett and a box of ammunition. I half expected to see six dummies set up at five-hundred and forty-two metres wearing body armour but no, they had been moved.

There were some guys down there with the Rangemaster target shooting and once that I clarified that I was testing for Charlie they were happy enough for me to shoot. The range is electronic, so the targets pop up when you need them rather than having squaddies in the butts pushing them up and down on frames. I put one up at five hundred metres and settled in with the weapon.

I calmed myself down as much as I could, I loved shooting and had never seen anything like this rifle. I loaded one round, took a deep breath, and gently squeezed the trigger, Shit this was a beast of a rifle, very loud and lots more kickback into my shoulder than my SA80 has.

Fortunately, many years ago I had fired the old Lee-Enfield, 303, the mainstay of WW2 and they kick like a mule, often causing deep painful bruises on your shoulder if you are not careful. This Barrett wasn't that bad, but you still have to treat it with respect.

Not sure where the round had gone, it could be in Wales by now, better switch on, I want these guys to think that I know what I am doing. I peered through the sight and yes I had missed the target, shit. Now I knew what to expect I reloaded took an even firmer grip, breathed out and fired. This time I saw the puff of dirt in the banking where the bullet had struck, it was low and to the right. Fine. My next shot I aimed off up a bit and to the left and hit it smack in the middle, result, just needed to tinker with the sights and we would be bang on.

That was the start of many happy hours on the various ranges as the designated tester for Charlie. The range staff soon got used to me showing up and just as on the pistol range would often give me advice and tips as to how I could improve.

19.

It was Friday afternoon and we were having our 3pm brew prior to disappearing for the weekend. We usually worked Saturdays but not this week, this was the weekend of 'The Wedding'. Alfie, one of the corporals in the team was getting married to his partner Sheila. They had been together for nine years and had two boys in junior school, they lived in a rented terraced house in the town and seemed to be fairly happy. I know, I know, why did they want to spoil that?

The October wedding had been planned with military precision which is an oxymoron if ever there was one, a bit like Military Intelligence-ha ha. Tonight was the stag do, the lads in the team and some of Alfie's civvy friends were all off to Bristol for a slap up Chinese meal and then a discreet, (Sheila didn't know) visit to a Gentleman's Club where they would be entertained by some young ladies who had allegedly forgotten to put their vests on.

Of course, I can't leave the base, but I wasn't stressed to not be going on the do, as strip clubs are not really my thing. I had been to a couple as a young squaddie and they left me a bit cold, a bit too impersonal but maybe that's just me.

One of the blades, a SAS sergeant named Big Mick, was a mate of Dougie's and he would be driving the minibus and was the designated driver / bodyguard so with a bit of luck all should go off fairly peacefully. Usually in the military anyone known as Big Mick would be a shortarse, army nicknames usually having only a tenuous relationship to reality or being a natural progression from someone's name.

My nickname was 'gunny' not because I was a US Marine Corps Gunnery Sergeant but because my name was Lewis hence, Lewis gun, Gunny. Anyway, back to Big Mick he was from Samoa or Fiji or some such place and he was massive, always smiling as well.

Tomorrow was the wedding with a church service and a reception at one of the nicer hotels in Hereford. It was costing the price of a small car but that was what Sheila wanted for her special day, Sheila and her family were Irish and some of her more boisterous relatives had been given a strongly worded warning from Sheila, her mum and her sisters about their behaviour.

Sunday was the after party at their house with relatives calling in for breakfast and the whole event gradually winding down as the guests started making their way home ready to start work on Monday morning.

This weekend had been carefully chosen for the wedding as we were not too busy, the only job coming up was a dozen Stryker armoured vehicles which were coming in on Monday and needing to be sorted by next Friday, we could manage that easily, even if most of the team had severe hangovers.

Dougies phone rang and he popped back into his office to answer it. The next thing we heard was, 'Fuck, fuck, fuck, fuck, fuck and fuck.' This from a guy who wasn't really comfortable saying 'shit'. He came back into the rec room and said,

'The Stryker's are coming in tonight, all twelve of them, they have to be out for 9am Monday. Bollocks.'

This was bad news for the wedding, prepping a Stryker takes a minimum of three hours, that's if it all goes well. Any reluctant bolts that won't budge or parts that don't fit exactly and you could easily add an hour onto that or even more. This was a disaster.

The team were divided in their focus on the key issues of this situation, two of them asking, 'What's Sheila going to say,' whilst the other two were wondering if they could still have the stag do and sort the vehicles out tomorrow. Dougie was sitting very still just muttering to himself. Time for me to step up.

'I can do them by Monday,'

'You can't do all of them,' Dougie said,

'Yes, I can mate, I can pull a couple of long days, we have all done it in Afghan and Iraq and at least now I've got a full workshop and none of them big fucking spiders crawling about.'

They have camel spiders in Iraq which are allegedly harmless but are about the size of a dinner plate and not my favourite creature. They used to come into the sheds over there to avoid the cold nights, just what you need when you crawl into a wagon first thing in the morning, yuck!

The lads were looking at each other.

'I can do it,' I repeated. 'I will get a flying start tonight, pull a long day tomorrow and Sunday and Bobs your uncle, Fanny's your aunt'

Dougie thought for a minute and then spoke, 'Ok have a go but if it's not cracked by lunchtime on Sunday you need to ring me and whoever is still standing will come in and give you a chuck out, yeah?'

'Yes, no worries, trust me with this.'

So, a very relieved wedding party made their way out of the sheds to prepare for their marathon booze and bints' weekend. Apparently, Sheila's younger sisters were very fond of squaddies and looking forward to meeting the lads from the team and vice versa.

That left me to set up.

I rang the gatehouse and the first wagons were due in at 4pm so by the time they had been through the quarantine process it would be at least a couple of hours after that before the motors got to me. Civvy lorries were not allowed in the camp so all vehicle deliveries had to be made to an off-base car park where they would be collected by our on-site transport team and brought down to our prep shed at the back of the workshop.

One feature I liked about this base is that all of the military vehicles were under cover at all times, it made sense really as we were a regular target for spy satellites and any movement could be spotted by those who had nefarious intent. This meant that the Strykers would start to arrive in the prep shed about 6pm before I could get my sticky little hands on them. Off to the mess then for tea and toast.

Back down to the shed and I got my first look at a Stryker. Impressive. They are an eight-wheeled, lightly armoured vehicle with a thirty-millimetre autocannon on the turret, not the Regiments usual style but these were for a special job which meant a weekends hard work for yours truly. They had to be winterised for a temperature of minus forty degrees C. We could not tell the manufacturer about this as there were very few places in the world that we would need vehicles with that capability, and it would have been a bit of a giveaway.

They were going up on the Finnish-Russian border with Finnish army markings and SAS teams working in Finnish army uniforms. The blades were going to be sneaking and peeking at the Russian forces on the border up there and if the worst happened, they would try to slow the soviets down for as long as they could. Very hush-hush.

These were the personnel carrier variants and the reason they had been chosen is that they can carry nine soldiers and a crew of two, this means that a four man SAS team could live in one and operate from it for an extended period of time in very adverse weather conditions. It would provide shelter, firepower if needed and an exit speed of up to sixty mph if the operation went to rat-shit as they so often do.

We needed to know about the mission because all of the vehicle bits that might be affected by severe cold had to be sorted. The anti-freeze obviously, but also all of the oils, some of the wiring, the battery, even the grease in some of the drive and steering joints plus some extra electrical bits had to be fitted. That's where the three hours came in. Great looking motor though.

    I moved the first three that arrived into our workshop and parked them over the pits so I could work underneath. I had to remove the bash plates first so I could reach the drain plugs and start the process. Shit they were heavy, involving me in some contortions with a special sliding jack we had rigged up. I started draining the fluids from the first one, then moved along the line. We had stacked the extra kit for them ready to start on Monday and that came in handy now as the batteries and various lubricants and other accessories were on individual trollies at the side of the shed.

    I cracked on with the first one, taking quite a bit of time with the electrical bits and the new super strength battery. I decided to do the same to the other two and got quicker as I practiced. I had inadvertently set up a little production line and it was going well. The anti-freeze was rated down to minus sixty as were the oils and the grease. Doing the same on each vehicle sped up the process but it was still past midnight when I finished. I thought of sacking it then but the thought of the team enjoying the attention of scantily clad young ladies seemed to spur me on. (not really).

So, I took a deep breath, moved the three I had finished to the handover area at the far side of the shed and lined the next three up on the pits. I sorted all of the drain plugs allowing the fluids to drain overnight and give me a flying start in the morning, not forgetting to hang one of our hand painted, 'fluids drained' signs on the front of each motor. Good workshop practice counts even when you are tired, in fact especially when you are tired -lol.

It was almost two o'clock when I got back to the mess, too tired to even have a drink I just stripped off and sacked out. Usual six o'clock start, I was tired, but I had been here before, in Afghan and Iraq we often worked twelve-hour shifts and even longer if there was still some work to do. I made some sausage and bacon butties to take for my lunch and headed back to the sheds.

Pleased now that I had done the extra last night the next three took until noon, that was six in the handover area and it was only Saturday lunchtime, I was happy with the progress so enjoyed a sandwich and a brew. Cracking on, the next three took just over six hours and I was knackered. I sat down in the crew room at just before eight and finished the last of my sandwiches. I was debating with myself whether to set the last three up to drain ready for tomorrow, but I decided against it. I was truly knackered which meant that I had more chance of making a mistake and I should have plenty of time on the Sunday.

Then a bloke wandered into the sheds, it was the CSM of the Mobility Troop the guys who were getting these vehicles on Monday. They would take care of the Finnish Army markings, sorting out the secure comms packages and supplying the ammunition which we were not authorised to hold. The wagons would then be put into containers whilst still under cover and shipped straight out to a Finnish Army base.

'Evening Sarge, how's it going?' He said, 'I'm Bill Murray, not the actor, have you got some Strykers for me?'

Wow, Bill Murray, not the actor, known as NTA, was a bit of a legend, he ran the Mobility Troop and was known as a bit of a hard case. Let me put that in context, if you are serving with the SAS regiment and you are known as a bit of a hard case then by all of the rules of normal society you are a very hard case indeed.

'Got nine done sir, ready to go.'

'On your own Sarge?'

'Yes sir, its Alfie's wedding so I offered to sort the trucks out.'

'You not invited to the wedding then?'

'No sir, I don't leave the base.'

'Oh, you're that Sergeant Smith'

'Yes sir.'

He looked at me for a moment, then came over and shook my hand.

He then asked the question I was most often asked about the siege.

'Why didn't you just shoot that paramedic woman?'

'She had a great arse sir; it would have been a waste.'

That was the answer I usually gave, and it seemed to satisfy most people, most men anyway.

He nodded, 'Good, so you have nine of them ready?'

'Yes sir, I should have the rest done by about one-ish tomorrow if there are no problems.'

'What if I needed the rest tonight?'

Shit, I was knackered now but if they needed them then I had better get started, better not bullshit this guy though. I looked at the clock.

'Possibly have them done by two am sir if all the bits fit.'

'Just testing Sarge, tomorrow will be fine.'

Sometimes I forgot how devious these guys were, I could have really messed up if I had started whingeing on about being tired.

'And you vouch for all these motors, do you?'

Testing time again but I had been around this block before, I always stuck to what we called the 'Titanic' principle, as used by the people of Belfast, in that – 'It was all right when it left here!'

Any problems with a motor after it left the shed was down to operator error not vehicle specialist incompetence.

I said nothing just looked at him. He paused for second then nodded.

'I'll send some guys over for these nine and get the rest about two-ish tomorrow if that suits?'

'That will be fine sir, gives me a bit of leeway if there's a problem.'

He nodded again, he was a vehicle guy and anyone who works with military vehicles knows that Trooper Murphy, (as in Murphy's Law) was never far away.

I drove the unit pickup back to the mess, I usually walked up but I was shattered. Grabbed a nice chicken curry from the standby hot plate and ate it in my room. One large Southern Comfort and I was fast asleep.

I felt much better on Sunday morning, decent breakfast, made some more sandwiches, back down the sheds, glad I had used the pickup last night as it was raining. By this time, I could have prepped a Stryker in my sleep so the last three were done by one o'clock. The other nine must have been collected last night so I just needed to pass these three over and it was a job well done.

I was halfway through a bacon sandwich when Dougie appeared carrying a bottle of champagne and a cardboard box. He looked a bit rough but had shown up just in case I needed a hand. True leadership in my opinion, not that common in the military surprisingly, which often seems to be a blame avoidance culture where shit rolls downhill, rather than management by example.

The weekend had gone well, the Gentlemen's Club being horrendously expensive and 'full of tarts.' Not sure what he was expecting, but I was very glad that I hadn't gone. The wedding itself had been fine, a bit of a fracas in the evening involving some of Sheila's cousins had seemed to be getting out of hand but luckily Big Mick and his wife had been invited and a few quiet words from him had worked a treat. A few quiet words from Big Mick usually did.

Dougie had brought me a bottle of champagne and a few pieces of wedding cake, sent in by Sheila in thanks for my covering for Alfie and the boys. Great stuff. We opened the champers and drank from our brew mugs, best lunch I have had for a while, bacon sarnie, wedding cake and champagne. Tasty.

Dougie nodded towards the sheds,

'Where's the rest of them?'

'NTA came round last night and took the nine I had ready.'

'Good, did he want the rest doing last night?'

'Yes, I offered but he said today was ok.'

'Next time tell him to fuck off or we will defect them all and they might get them by Christmas.'

Fair enough I suppose, as Dougie was the team manager he had to be able to hold his own in a high-pressure environment full of people who wanted stuff doing yesterday. If we defect a vehicle it doesn't move until we say so, a technique I had used once when a young infantry lieutenant was being a twat to one of my team. His Warrior personnel carrier was defected by me and we sat on it for a week until he got the message, reappeared with a case of beer for the lads and his wagon was suddenly much better.

Just then three guys from the Mob Troop showed up, one of them carrying a case of Stella Artois,

'Thank you from NTA' he said, popping the beer in our fridge.

'Cheers mate,' I said, 'Thank him very much.'

They walked off to collect the motors which thankfully all fired up straight away, then they were out of the shed and no longer my problem. Result.

'I've been here four years,' Dougie said, 'We've never had any beer from anyone, you must have impressed him.'

'Yes, he was probably so relieved that I didn't tell him to fuck off and come back at Christmas.' Oh, we did laugh.

'Seriously though Mike, you have done us all a big favour this weekend, you are off the clock now until Wednesday afternoon, just come back in for the footy.'

Well I was very knackered now and starting to feel the effects of the late nights and the champagne,

'Cheers boss,'

Back to the mess, very pleasant afternoon doze and I enjoyed my evening meal.

So dear reader you ask why I have been banging on about random military vehicles, well it is my job and I enjoy it but it's also very relevant as to what happened on Monday morning. Stay tuned.

20.

You will remember that when I first arrived on the camp, I had received a brown envelope with one hundred pounds in marked, 'Naafi Money.' I continued to receive one every week and had got used to visiting the Naafi every Sunday morning, it was a quiet time to shop as most of the guys were at church. (not really).

The Naafi on the camp was a comprehensive full-service shop, they would order stuff from Amazon for us and any other mail order retail service, without our having to give personal details, just pay the Naafi staff in advance and your stuff would be there the next week. Handy for me as I bought books and DVD's. I also had a liking for Rohan clothing since volunteering for adventure training courses in what now seemed like a lifetime ago. Once viewed, books and DVD's would be left in the rec room at the mess where an informal library system had operated for years.

Having played 'Sort the Strykers' all weekend it was now Monday morning when I went shopping and there were quite a few civvies around. No worries, after a pleasant walk down the hill I called in to pick up a book I had ordered, restock on crisps, nuts and biscuits and a bottle of Southern Comfort. I alternated weekly between SC, Bombay Sapphire Gin and my usual twelve pack of Stella. No, I'm not an alcoholic, I'm just a drunk so I don't have to go to all the meetings-lol.

I was walking away from the shop with a carrier bag in each hand when a woman's voice said,

'Michael?'

I turned around and she slapped me across the face hard, this was a full power, teeth rattling slap, shit. Lisa.

The combat part of my brain swung into overdrive, I leaned back to avoid the next slap and with my hands full I was planning to kick her in the knee, I never got the chance though as she grabbed me and was hugging me and crying. Talk about mixed messages?

She was very upset, sobbing into my chest, I slowly put the shopping bags down and put my arms around her. She felt good and she smelt good.

'I thought I'd never see you again, what are you doing here?'

I took a deep breath, my face was still stinging,

'Colin Warner got me out, he thought I would be more use here.'

'It is so good to see you, I tried to write to you, but they said nothing was getting through,'

'Why did you slap me then?'

She leaned away from me slightly and poked me in the chest with her finger.

'That was for raping me that first time at the siege, the other times not so much but that first time was wrong, and you deserved a slap.'

Couldn't argue with that really so I just said,

'Strange times,'

'Yes, it was.'

So, we sat on a bench outside the Naafi and she told me that her husband Max had been a captain in the regiment and he had been killed overseas two years ago. She managed the Family's Support system here at the camp and the army had let her stay on in her job and also let her stay in their quarter (army speak for a house). She had been doing fine since his death until she met a randy vehicle specialist in a police station far, far away. She seemed to be a bit happier now she had slapped me and I was very glad that I didn't kick her in the knee.

I told her the edited highlights of my trial and incarceration glossing over the midnight car boot escape just saying that Colin had arranged my 'posting' to the camp and adding that I didn't leave the base.

She had to get back to work and asked if I would like to come for tea at her house tonight, she was cooking spag bol and I hadn't had a home cooked meal since the last decade. My previous girlfriends had not been chosen for their cooking ability if you know what I mean-lol.

She gave me the address, and said,

'It's just a meal, I am not going to have sex with you.'

'In that case I am not going to shoot you in the head'

She laughed at that, fair enough.

I was walking back up to the mess when a thought suddenly struck me. I was so overwhelmed that I had to go and sit on a wall, I'm not saying I was having the shakes again, but my breathing was definitely a bit ragged. Lisa was regiment.

That meant that the women and children at the siege were regiment women and kids. Shit. That was why they had come for me, that was why I was so welcome in the mess and that was why Colin had asked me about the library when he saw me back at Colchester. I don't grass anybody up ever but he would be an experienced interrogator, get a few beers down me, build some rapport and then at the end ask me about the library. He must have heard some whispers and wanted to see if I would gossip about it, the second question that he asked about Trooper Morgan was just a smokescreen. So if I had answered that one question about the library differently I would probably still be sitting in a little room at the CTC thinking about the next forty-five years. Scary.

The guys here must have been going crazy that their families were stuck in the siege with just a mortar team and a vehicle wonk looking after them. They had no way of knowing that the vehicle wonk was about to turn into Colonel Kurtz from Apocalypse Now and start practising total war on the enemy. That's why we got Apaches and Paras to relieve us. Wow!

I must have looked so rough that a young lad going past in a Land-rover stopped and asked if I was ok. I told him I was thanks, I told him that I had just had a few too many beers last night. He gave me a lift back to the mess and I opened a can of Stella and went for a lie down. The thought that my entire future could have rested on one answer to that one question was a bit of a shock really.

Fortunately, I had never visited the library and wouldn't know any of the women if I bumped into them in the future. I did wonder if the RSM's wife had been in the library and he hated the thought of me knowing what she had been up to, I thought about it for a while and then decided no and that he was probably just a twat.

Later that afternoon being the suave sophisticated chap that I am I called in at the Naafi for a bottle of their finest screw top white wine, almost seven quid a bottle and presented myself at Lisa's pleasant little house on one of the family accommodation streets at the bottom end of the camp. Nice Volvo estate on the drive, I'm a vehicle guy so sue me for noticing.

She looked relaxed and happy when she opened the door. She was wearing jeans, trainers, and a shirt top. (GAFS definitely), she looked at the wine and said,

'You shouldn't have,'

'Just a token,' I said,

'No really you shouldn't have that's awful wine.'

Your welcome, I thought but just made a joke of it.

Any way the meal was very pleasant we talked about the siege, carefully avoiding the whole, 'fuck me or I won't shoot you affair', and it became clear that it was only after we were rescued that she had realised how close we had come to being overrun.

'Were you really going to shoot me?'

'Yes, just walk straight into the room and do it so you didn't have time to be scared,'

'How close were you to doing it?'

'A few minutes really, I didn't want to leave it to the last second in case I got hit,'

'Did you really fix bayonets?'

'Yes,'

Why do people keep asking me that?

As I was leaving, she saw me to the door and said,

'I would like to do this again, why don't you give me a ring during the week and we can arrange something for next weekend, we can just see what happens yes?'

That was fine with me I wasn't going anywhere, she gave me a piece of paper with her number on, then there was a little awkward moment until she leaned forward and kissed me on the cheek. Still, better than getting slapped on it believe me.

21.

On the Tuesday, I was sitting in the rec room after breakfast trying to find anything interesting to read in the day's papers. One of the mess staff came in and told me that Major Warner wanted to see me. He didn't say when but a summons from JB (how does Major Colin Warner end up with the nickname of JB? Simple really, he was the Operations Officer, the OO, -007- James Bond-JB-!) meant as soon as.

I took five minutes to slip my uniform on, can't show up at his office in a track suit. The Ice Queen was Colins admin person a very pretty blonde captain who treated all of the other ranks like shit. It was estimated that you would have to be at least a General to get into her knickers but despite her looks I am not sure I would bother. She was the sort of woman you would shag once just to say that you had done and then not call her in the morning. I would imagine that she definitely could not take a joke.

The biggest joke on her was the TVS, the 'Tit-view seats,' there were several seats for people waiting to see Colin outside of his office and a couple of them gave you a great view of her tits under her tight white blouse which she was not aware of because the computer monitor blocked her view. Funny or what?

She was at her desk outside his office and had the usual miserable expression on her face. I wondered if I could introduce her to the CSI woman from Colchester, they could have had a right laugh on a night out together.

'You can go in,' IQ said,

At least with JB he didn't keep you hanging around.

I entered the office and stood to attention,

'Relax Michael, just a quickie, Lisa Carstairs is off limits, ok?'

The only answer that was ever acceptable in this office with this officer was,

'Yes sir.'

There was no way I would ever ask why; I didn't need to know why, or he would have told me and in any case the man had saved me from a forty-five-year prison sentence so whatever he wanted he got.

I went back to the mess and did wonder what the problem was with Lisa but it was not really a problem for me I would just not ring her. She would get the message and JB would be happy. Result.

Well, result until about 11am on Friday morning when Dougie popped his head round the door and told me I had a visitor. I was up to my elbows in a Yamaha dirt bike we were trying to prep for the Mobility troop to break so I wandered out into the reception area and found Lisa, smiling, but in that way women have that tells you they are not happy.

'Have you lost my number; just thought I would check in as I hadn't heard from you?'

Faced with a pissed off woman I am afraid it was every man for himself, JB was big enough and ugly enough to take the flak.

'Major Warner had me in on Tuesday morning, he told me you were off limits.'

'Off limits, why would I be off limits? It's nothing to do with him, it's not like we are getting married or are a security risk or anything?'

As usual when faced with this type of situation I found it better to keep my mouth firmly shut, they could sort it out between them but at the moment the prospect of another spectacular blow job seemed to be receding into the distance.

'Off limits, why would I be off limits?'

I have seen people die, I have seen people badly injured and I have seen people grieving in horrible situations all over this globe of ours but I sincerely hope that I never see again the look of anguish on a person's face that I saw on Lisa's face as she worked out why she was off limits.

'He's not dead.' Shit I thought.

'It's Max, the bastards not dead.'

Then she was gone and I heard her Volvo screeching out of the car park.

I heard later that she had gone straight up to the HQ block, told the Ice Queen to 'Fuck off' when she had tried to stop her going in and apparently the yelling from JB's office could be heard all over the building. Not good.

About half-an-hour later Dougie gave me the good news,

'JB wants you.' Oh crap.

One wrong move and I could be on a boat back to Colchester, well not a boat but you know what I mean.

'Go straight in,' said the IQ, still looking like a bulldog who had swallowed a wasp.

'Michael, just a quickie, Lisa Carstairs is now not off limits,'

'Yes sir,'

'And God help you.'

'Yes sir.'

Not sure why I needed God's help, technically I hadn't done anything wrong, but you know what women are like, I could well end up getting the blame for whatever had gone wrong just because I was the closest?

So, did I want to ring her and see her again, especially if she was as pissed-off as I suspected that she was going to be? Was it really my business or could I just keep quiet, let things settle down and stay away from the Naafi on Mondays?

I thought about it, one result of my shitty childhood is that I value loyalty above everything else. One of the great things about the army is that you are prepared to fight to the death for people you don't even like, and they will fight to the death for you.

You may have arguments and even punch ups with other squaddies but the minute that the enemy start lobbing ordnance in your direction then you are all brothers in arms. I could not imagine the feeling of betrayal for Lisa if her husband was not actually dead and that there were people on the camp who knew about it.

I went straight back to the mess and found a phone.

'Lisa, hi its Michael, just been told that you are not off limits anymore, how are you doing?'

'They let me think he was dead, we had a funeral, I grieved for him. I stayed away from other men until you ripped my knickers off, the bastard is living in Guatemala with another woman and their baby.'

Shit, she was slurring her words a bit but I couldn't really blame her for getting pissed. She had mentioned at the siege that she could not have children and that Max had been OK with it. She insisted on condoms with me because 'she did not know where I had been'.

I took a deep breath, I am not really a people person as you may have guessed,

'Is there anything I can do?'

'You can come round tonight and get pissed with me,'

Sounds like a plan,

'What time?'

'About eight, not doing food just booze and don't bring any more of that shitty wine.'

'OK see you then.'

That went better than I expected, I would take her a bottle of Dr Bombay's finest Sapphire gin and all her problems would disappear at least until the morning.

The evening was a little cool so I was wearing my leather jacket over a polo shirt and jeans. I had an unopened bottle of gin in the room so I took that with me. I knocked on her door and got the second big surprise of the day.

She was wearing a frilly black negligee over the full kit of black basque, stockings and suspenders, I nearly came in my pants, wow!

'Will you come in and fuck me?'

She was very drunk no need for the Bombay tonight.

I followed her in, and she went up the stairs to her bedroom, the curtains were closed and a scented candle was burning on a tray.

At this point I would suggest that any women readers move on to the next chapter whilst I have a word with the guys.

Guys here's the deal. If you ever get chance to have sex with a woman who is very, very angry, but who is not actually angry at you, then go for it, she was amazing.

She took the lead and was very assertive with me. I lay on my back and she did all kinds of positions. I enjoyed 'Cowgirl,' where she more or less sat on my cock and writhed up and down and then she did 'Reverse Cowgirl' which was facing the other way. What's the point of that I thought, at least with 'cowgirl' you can play with her tits but with the reverse position you are just looking at her back?

She was very, very wet and that was helping me last longer as it was diluting the usual contact between cock and pussy. I was breathing a bit fast as she was certainly fitter than I was and seemed to have more stamina. She then wanted to do it doggy style which I always enjoy but then she told me to tell her when I was coming. I felt the usual stirrings and let her know.

'Finish off up my bum,' she said. Wow!

It's a long time since I had been invited to use the tradesman's entrance and on that occasion it was only because we were both very drunk and had run out of condoms. Wow, what a thrill.

'Be gentle, but I want you to come in my arse,'

Yes ma'am I thought, fortunately the condom was very wet because she was very wet so I lined my dick up and slowly slipped it into her arse. She gave a bit of a gasp, I reached out and took some of her hair in each hand and slowly pulled her head back so that she was arching her spine.

I had heard the guys talk about doing this and that it tightened up the woman's arse muscles and gave you a better ride, it did. Then she started wriggling her hips and that was me done. Wow. She collapsed onto the bed and I slipped out and tried to slow my breathing down, I was wondering what had just happened.

I cleaned us both up with some wipes and she started sobbing, deep racking sobs as she was lying face down on the bed. I lay down and put my arm around her and there was just nothing I could say, the love of her life, and the people she trusted most in the army had betrayed her how do you come back from that?

After about twenty minutes she had stopped crying and her breathing had settled down, I thought she was asleep but she said,

'Will you go now please?'

'Ok.'

I slipped off the bed and got dressed, the candle was still burning so I could see her body, and I have to say she looked amazing.

'Will you phone me Wednesday or Thursday just so we can talk?'

'Yes, I will phone on Wednesday, before the footy, whatever happens.'

If JB wants me to ditch her now, then he is going to be shit out of luck.

I went downstairs feeling a bit sad and a bit angry really, I have been crapped on many times in my life but never as badly as that.

22.

I slipped my leather jacket on and quietly closed the door. It was dark now and I walked to the end of the street finding my way carefully in the dim street lighting. This was another way we tried to keep information from the spy satellites, not sure it was working, it was certainly not working for me.

I reached the end of the street and two guys came out from behind a hedge, they were wearing combat jackets and jeans but more worryingly for me they were wearing ski masks of the type you see bank robbers using. I stopped about ten feet away from them.

'What's up guys?'

'You're what's up pal,' said the shorter of the two who was standing on the left.

He said it in a Scottish accent, not the nice one that makes you think of fine whisky and long mountain views but the harsher one that makes you think of inner-city Glasgow and places you would not visit in the dark.

'You've been dipping your wick in somebody else wife, pal.'

Well that's an expression I hadn't heard in a few years, but he was obviously mistaken.

'You need to talk to Major Warner guys, you need to get up to date,'

'We don't need ta talk ta no fucker,' he said and produced a large hunting knife from inside his jacket.

Oh Shit. I took another two steps towards them. Best not to show fear.

'We're going to slice up your little cock, so you won't be sticking it in any more married fanny,'

'You have got the wrong information guys, you need to talk to Major Warner,'

'No fucking way, we will just fuck you up so you can't fuck her up.'

They both laughed at that clever word play, that's when I pulled the revolver out of my jacket and shot him through the left knee tracked the barrel a fraction to the right and shot his mate through his right knee. The second guy hadn't said anything but he had come to do me harm so he was included. Guilty by association I'm afraid.

They both fell to the ground like someone who had been shot through the knee at close range by a small revolver firing some very special, US police issue, Teflon-coated ammunition. Understandable really.

Why was I carrying a revolver? Well a couple of weeks after I had arrived I went to see Colin and explained that I had thought about my future and I was not going back to prison. He understood this and agreed that I could carry a sidearm of my choice promising that if I was ever being sent back to Colchester he would let me know by a codeword we had agreed on and I would find a quiet place and arrange my own exit.

Anyway, back to the two jock idiots who were now writhing on the ground. The gobby one was screaming about what he was going to do to me until I walked up to him forced his head down to the ground with the pistol barrel and asked him to tell me again, he became very quiet at that point and pissed himself.

I left him where he was and took the mobile phone out of my other pocket, switched it on and pressed the speed dial button. It only had one number in, the control room here at Hereford. Two rings and a voice said, 'Zero'

I gave him my location, brief details of the incident and asked him to inform Sierra Two which is Major Warner's callsign. This situation had all the makings of a total clusterfuck as I had just shot two SAS troopers on the main SAS base having spent the evening enjoying the sexual favours of a woman who some people clearly thought was still married to an SAS officer.

The first car to arrive was an MOD Police car crewed by a young constable who looked to be about twelve but was probably in his early twenties. He got out of the car and was clearly in a bit of a state because he shouted at me,

''Get down on the ground,'

'No,'

I had put the gun back in my pocket, I was not agitated or threatening anybody and anyway he was Mod Plod not Military Police or I might have been a bit more interested.

He then lost the plot even further,

'Warning, if you do not get down on the ground, I will draw my taser,'

One way and another this had been a really intense evening and my usually tiny reservoir of patience was completely exhausted.

'Fuck off you pillock.'

He then grabbed the Taser from his belt, pointed it at me and yelled,

'Taser, Taser, Taser.'

Enough is enough, I pulled the pistol from my pocket, pointed it at his balls and shouted,

'Pistol, pistol, pistol. If you shoot me with that taser my finger will twitch and I will shoot you in the bollocks, think about it pillock months in hospital, lots of pain and no chance of any little mod plod kiddies anywhere in your future.'

I could see he was thinking about it but fortunately for both of us the big Jag showed up and Colin walked around the back of the police car towards us.

'Put your Taser down officer,'

'Sir, this man has a weapon,'

'Yes, and he has just shot two of my soldiers so he has nothing to lose by shooting you in the bollocks. Put the Taser away now.'

The copper made the wisest choice of his young life and put his Taser back in its holster.

Colin then went up to him and had a quiet conversation probably along the lines of 'this never happened, and you were never here.' I imagine that happened a lot on this camp.

The police car pulled away and Colin came up to me. I repeated the details of the incident I had given to Zero. This was not a guy who appreciated bullshit.

He looked across at the two on the ground,

'Take your masks off,'

They did.

'Dumb and dumber' he said, 'Two idiots from mob troop.'

He thought for a minute and then asked me for the pistol. I handed it to him butt first.

'How many rounds left?'

'Three,'

'Good,'

He then turned and shot each of the soldiers once in the head. Shit.

I said nothing.

'Four people can keep a secret,' He said.

I knew the end of this phrase and its 'If three of them are dead,' and there was one round left in that pistol.

He smiled at me,

'If two of them are dead and one of them is wanted for war crimes,'

He handed me the gun back. Whew!

'They wouldn't have kept their mouths shut; we would have binned them from the regiment but they would have blabbed about us housing a war criminal. More than that though, this place only works, only ever works because we fight for each other. I brought you onto this base and you are under my protection, fuck what the RSM thinks.'

Fair enough, it had been a strange day since Lisa showed up at the sheds this morning and I was ready for my bed.

'How is Mrs Carstairs?' He asked,

'Don't expect a Christmas card.'

He laughed and shrugged his shoulders.

'What could we do, Max is on a very secret mission and we had to stage his death to protect him and her, what else could we do?'

Fuck, I see his point. Of course that left me as usual between a rock and a hard place holding the shitty end of the stick whilst standing on very thin ice.

'Time to disappear,' he said, 'This was a tragic training accident and you were never here.'

'Yes sir.'

Back to the mess and had the shakes for a few minutes, reloaded the pistol and slept with it on my bedside table and a chair jammed under the door handle.

Eating breakfast next morning I was joined by NTA who now had two fewer troopers than he had last night.

'You may not have heard sarge, but we lost two guys in a tragic training accident last night.'

I said nothing.

'Their families will get full benefits and pensions of course.'

Still nothing from me.

'Major Warner and myself have spoken to the troops and explained that the accident occurred because the troopers were mistaken about some information and did not come to me or any of the troop NCO's to check it out.'

I waited.

'All of my troopers are very clear about the situation going forward. There is no chance of this type of accident happening in the future.'

In his roundabout way I think he was telling me that I was ok.

'Are we good then sir?'

'Yes Sergeant we are good and I know that you did not slot them, you were just defending yourself.'

'Thank you, sir.'

Down at the sheds later, Dougie called me into his office, closed the door and said,

'What the fuck happened?'

Dougie was a great bloke, but he also loved to gossip, as most soldiers do.

'I have no knowledge of anything that might or might not have taken place at any location, anywhere at any time.'

I looked him in the eyes as I said this, and I think he got the message.

'Shit mate.' He said, 'Are you fucked now?'

'I have been told that as nothing happened anywhere at any time involving me that there will be no repercussions of any kind going forward.'

'Well that sounds like NTA,' he said, 'So I guess we will be OK. Just in case,' He opened his desk drawer and took out a Browning pistol.

'Ten in the mag and one in the breech, mags swapped once a week so the springs don't settle,'

Shit, serious firepower, the magazines do take thirteen rounds, but a wise soldier never loads a magazine to its maximum, that is just asking for Trooper Murphy to show up when you really don't want him to.

'Help yourself if you need it. If they come for you make sure you injure them not kill them, if they are injured it involves medics and records and somebody might ask questions.'

'Thanks boss.'

'You're welcome, now let's see if we can go and fuck up some motorbikes.'

Begs the question though, why did Dougie keep a loaded weapon in his drawer?

23.

I rang Lisa on the Wednesday; she was very quiet on the phone and asked if we could start again just being friends. I knew what that meant but I didn't mind if I could offer her a little bit of support after everything that we and she had been through, then I would be happy without any sexual component. Basically, we had two false starts and sitting watching a DVD might be good for both of us.

I went round that evening with my trusty pistol in my pocket and two speed-loaders of five rounds each in my other pocket, once bitten etc. Anyone appearing from behind a hedge tonight would have a big shock coming.

She was very quiet and we ate a steak and asparagus dinner in silence. She loosened up a bit as we watched a movie, 'Deadpool,' her choice but I loved it. As I was leaving she came in for a cuddle and said,

'I have been thinking, would you like to stay over on Saturday, chill out on Sunday and stay for lunch?'

Would I ever? But I thought I had better be clear about the arrangements.

I pulled her close and whispered in her ear,

'Where would I be sleeping?'

'In my bed with me,'

'Doesn't that make you very vulnerable?'

'Why?'

'Well suppose I wake up in the middle of the night and want to have sex, what would happen then?'

She realised where I was going with this and started to play along.

'Well I would have no pants on, just my nightie so I suppose I would have to have sex with you, just to be polite.'

This was turning me on. I shifted slightly so that she wouldn't feel my erection against her body. I thought I would push things a little further.

'Suppose I wake up in the middle of the night and want to have kinky or unusual sex with you what then?'

'Well then I guess we would have to negotiate wouldn't we?'

Roll on Saturday, I left with a slight limp and managed to make it back to the mess without shooting anyone or scaring the shit out of any young coppers.

I turned up on Saturday night with a Naafi carrier bag with another bottle of gin, a toothbrush, and some spare clothes in. There was no way that the neighbours would know that there was anything unusual in the bag although by lunchtime tomorrow anyone in the camp who was interested would know that I had spent the night.

Lisa met me at the door wearing a pretty summer dress not the black basque, shame.

'Can we save it till we go to bed, be just like a normal couple?'

'Yes of course,' although we were about as far from a normal couple as you could get and it felt like a more sensitive reply than,

'No, Mrs. get your kit off.'

We had a very pleasant evening, finger food and gin, she turned out to be a fan of country music as I am and she had a much better collection than me so we sat and listened to Kris, John, Willie and Waylon as well as some of the newer stuff that I hadn't heard before.

Eventually she said, 'Bedtime,' turning the word into an invitation, at least in my mind.

'Listen, no pressure, I am quite happy to go back to the mess if you have changed your mind?'

The last thing I wanted to do was stay if she had changed her mind, this woman had suffered enough.

"I haven't changed my mind, I want someone to sleep next to and wake up with, I haven't done that for some time.'

'I can do that.'

We went upstairs and I slipped into her bed naked. She came back from the bathroom and turned the light out from outside, she then came into the room wearing just a skinny nightie that just about came down to her hips, there was enough light for me to see that she had nothing underneath.

I felt weird, I had slept over with a few women but not like this it felt strange. She slipped under the covers and lay on her side of the bed. I did not really know what to do, the last time we had been in this room she had taken the lead and been very demanding, I have no problem with repeating that but this time it was different.

She was lying on my left, so I reached out and took her right hand and put it on my cock. She held it for a minute and then began to stroke me.

'Can we just do this?' she said.

'If you want.'

As I said, I felt weird and this was uncharted territory for me. She rolled towards me and began to use both hands. I kissed her and she kissed me back and then I was coming in her hand and we both stopped moving. Wow.

She went to wash her hands in the bathroom and I rolled onto my back to try and avoid dripping on her sheets, ever the gentleman. She came back in and snuggled into me backwards so her arse was pressed against my stomach, been there done that I thought, not maliciously though and we fell asleep.

I woke up to the sound and smell of bacon frying, is there a better way to wake up? I dressed quickly, brushed my teeth, and went downstairs to the kitchen.

'Sorry about last night, I wasn't up for a full session,'

'No worries,' What else could I say, you know I can't talk to women.

She came to me for a kiss and then went back to cooking the bacon, very domestic but after life in the mess, very pleasant.

'Tea in the pot,'

And there was, result.

So we hung out, as the young people say and I left mid-afternoon. Again, no one waiting in ambush for me and I made it back to my room unscathed.

We had agreed for me to go for tea on Wednesday and sleepover again the next Saturday. I think she needed to have some sort of routine for what was happening and I was quite happy to oblige.

Wednesday was a meal, a movie, and a goodnight kiss. Saturdays were a sleepover with benefits and a cooked breakfast, definitely better than an ASDA all day breakfast sandwich.

24.

It was early evening and I was sitting in the rec room having a cup of tea before going in for my food. The RSM came rushing in, saw me and said,

'Are you any good with that Barrett?'

Not a time for self-deprecation.

'Yes sir, 100 per cent up to one thousand metres.'

I hadn't fired it beyond that distance as I didn't go off the base but at one thousand metres I hit what I shot at.

'Grab one and some ammo from the armoury, I will tell Charlie, helipad in fifteen minutes, full tactical, do not carry anything in your pockets.'

'Yes sir.'

I moved, it seemed like somebody was in the shit somewhere and they were desperate for some sniper cover. I'm not supposed to leave the base but if the guys were in trouble then I was there.

Full combat gear, Charlie was waiting at the armoury with the Barrett in its big plastic carrying case. He gave me a box of mixed rounds, some tracer and some standard so I could load for the task. Down to the helipad at the bottom of the camp and there were five troopers standing near an unmarked Blackhawk which was 'turning and burning'. This shit was for real.

Shrek was standing there by the chopper and he was searching everyone who was boarding. He gave me a thorough pat down and then nodded for me to get on.

We all had headsets and the RSM briefed us that he was going to drop me on a ridge line overlooking a country road and the rest of the team were going to stop a truck further up the road. He did not say why. If the truck got as far as my position, I was to stop it with the rifle ideally without killing the driver.

Fair enough, I was very excited to be out on operations again, I had thought that those days were over. We flew for about twenty minutes and the chopper circled over a wooded hill when the RSM pointed out the road and direction the truck would be travelling in. If the lads missed it the chopper would call me on the radio with the instructions to fire.

They dropped me in a clearing about five hundred metres from the site. I lugged the big case to the firing point and set up the rifle. Ten rounds in the special issue magazine, tracer first then every third one with tracer for the last two. I would be counting shots anyway, but two consecutive tracers would tell me it was time to change mags. I loaded a second mag with the same mix and settled down to wait.

I was pleased in a way that they had asked me to get involved, maybe the RSM was warming to my presence on the camp or maybe he was just desperate?

You get to be good at waiting in the army which is handy because I was there for hours. Very little activity on the road and no trucks. I was getting cold but I didn't mind. Finally, I heard a radio call telling me to be at the exfil site in five minutes.

I repacked the rifle in its case, left the mags loaded as I could sort them out later and sprinted back to the clearing. The chopper came in fast and low, the RSM was leaning out of the door, I put the case in and the chopper started to lift, he held his hand out to me and I took it and started up the steps. The aircraft was about ten feet off the floor when he leaned back, let go of my hand and kicked me in the chest. Shit.

I fell on my back and was really winded. I rolled on to my face to avoid the debris that was being kicked up by the downdraft and gasped for breath. The chopper was up and gone and I was on my own in the dark. I stumbled up and staggered across to the nearest trees for some cover, shit, shit, shit. It was a setup. Bastard.

I went into the trees and found a spot to sit down whilst I got my breath back. This was quite an elaborate set up leaving me miles from anywhere with no money and no id. I sat for a few minutes and it did not seem as if anyone was coming to investigate the helicopter. I didn't know where I was and had no survival gear.

Never worry, I had spent lots of time in dark forests on a variety of training exercises in this country and abroad and was not stressed by the darkness or the isolation. I sat and listened carefully until I heard running water and headed for the stream, streams go downhill and often have paths alongside or near them.

I followed the stream and carefully made my way a few hundred metres down the hill to a road and paused for a look around. I could see a glow in the sky indicating a town off to the right and I set off towards it at a steady jog. First thing I needed was a motor.

I reached the outskirts of the small town which had a welsh road sign that I didn't recognise. As I wandered through the buildings there was no one about which was fine by me. Then, bingo a post office. Closed and locked of course but sitting outside it was Postman Pats favourite, a little red post van. What can you drive around in the middle of the night without attracting attention? Yes, a little red post van. We had some at the camp along with a selection of other utility vans and trucks which the blades used for surveillance.

This was when my truly suspicious nature really paid off. Duct-taped to the back of my right calf, which no-one checks during a pat-down search, was a small device I had collected from the sheds on my way to the armoury. Basically, it looks like a large car key but it will open and disarm the alarm of any vehicle on the roads today. Very hush-hush but of course we had some in the sheds and I had one in my hand now.

I opened the van and found a hi-vis waist coat with 'post office' on the back which I put on, great stuff, better than Harry Potters invisibility cloak. Even better was that it was a new van and it had a sat-nav, result. I fired it up, it was full of diesel, I typed

Hereford into the sat-nav and off we went. The roads were very quiet at this time of night, I did see one police car going the other way, but the coppers waved at me and I waved back, no problem.

After about an hour I reached the outskirts of Hereford and by then I had time to concoct my cunning plan. If it worked as planned then I could fuck the RSM and I wouldn't have to buy him dinner first. I drove into town, found a phone box and got the operator to phone Lisa, reversing the charge.

'Michael?'

The operator had given her my name when she asked her to pay for the call.

'Hi, I'm in town and I need a ride back in to camp on the quiet if possible?'

She thought for a moment, this woman had been married to a special forces captain for a long time so no unnecessary questions and no messing, she just said.

'McDonalds, fifteen minutes.'

'Thanks.'

I drove around the town to the post office where I left the van alongside several others and locked it up. Somebody would have a puzzle in the morning but there was no evidence of a break in, just a few extra miles on the clock. I left the jacket on and walked up to Maccy D's trying to look like a postal worker on his way home.

    I figured it was best to hide in plain sight so I sat on one on of the benches outside the restaurant, which was drive-through only at this time of night. The last time I had a Mac's was at the CTC when Colin had brought me burgers and beer and to be honest I was hoping that Lisa would bring some money with her as I had missed my evening meal and was getting a bit peckish. The big Volvo came into the car park and stopped. I walked over got in the passenger seat and kissed her.

    'Thanks for coming out, PD conned me into a helicopter ride then kicked me out.'

    'Bastard,' she said.

    'Can you get me back in without anyone knowing, I have a cunning plan.'

    'Just go to the gatehouse, get them to call Colin and tell him what happened, PD will be in the shit.'

    'Can we do that if all else fails, but I would like to try and sneak back in if possible?'

    'OK, I promised the guard on the back gate a Big Mac, would you like one?'

Would I ever? Apparently, there was a back gate used by families and civvy staff which was less heavily guarded than the main gate. After Max had supposedly died Lisa had often done a McDonalds run in the middle of the night when she couldn't sleep, just for something to do and she would usually bring a burger back for the gate guard.

Three big Macs and a strawberry milkshake (for me) later and we were off towards the camp. My burger took three bites and I was still slurping the milkshake when Lisa pulled into a lay-by. I got in the boot under the luggage cover and we drove up to the camp. Second time I had done this I thought.

She had a brief chat with the guy on the gate, gave him his burger and then we were in. Sorted.

I had asked her to drop me at the back of the sheds where it was unlit and not covered by any security cameras as I had one more part of my little plan to sort.

There were night lights burning in the sheds and they were unlocked as usual. We may need to start things up quickly in an emergency and faffing about looking for the shed keys would not be a good idea. I had left the hi-vis jacket in Lisa's car and was just about invisible in my combat gear but in any event, I was a soldier walking around an army base in uniform, again invisible.

I found the small device I wanted and then went looking for the RSM's car. He had a black Golf GTI with all the goodies on and he was very proud of it. He had his own designated parking space on the approach to the mess and that's where I found it. I pointed my little device at the car and pressed the button, there was no light or sign of anything happening but that was by design. The device simply scrambled the cars immobiliser system making it impossible to start and the effect could only be fixed by a VW main dealer.

I had once seen a motto on a barracks wall that said,

'In Defeat Malice - In Victory Revenge'   Words to live by.

And so to bed.

The next morning I was in for breakfast bright and early and chose my cutlery carefully.

After about ten minutes PD came into the room followed as always by Shrek. He was about halfway to the counter when he saw me, did a double take and then stormed over to where I was sitting.

'What the fuck are you doing here? He screamed.

The rest of the room went very quiet.

'Eating breakfast sergeant-major,'

I said loudly, so that everyone could hear. Sometimes you need witnesses.

'I have checked the gate logs, how the fuck did you get back on this camp?'

This was when my little plan clicked into place.

'I am not allowed to leave this camp sergeant-major under any circumstances, by order of the Commanding Officer. Why would I need to get back in?'

Checkmate arsehole. He could not discipline me for sneaking back in without revealing how I had got out. Everyone in the mess was now realising that something was amiss and I am sure he would be todays target for the serious rumour squad that operated throughout the camp.

I thought he was going to explode but sadly he didn't, he walked off and Shrek leaned over my table, as it was early I was sitting alone. He began to tell me that I was in serious trouble and then he stopped. I had chosen a serrated steak knife from the cutlery drawer and out of sight of the rest of the room I was pressing the point into his groin just near the big femoral artery. One flick of my wrist and he would be having a very bad day. I am pretty sure they would get him to the med centre before he bled to death but it was not guaranteed, he didn't have many friends in this room.

He stopped threatening me and I said quietly,

'You can be number seven hundred and eighty-two, I have nothing to lose.'

He was looking into my eyes and I am fairly sure that he could see that I was serious and I was, if he so much as twitched, I would bury the blade into his leg.

'I will fucking get you, one dark night you twat,'

'Whenever you are ready Shrek.'

He hated that name and had threatened to punch anyone who used it. I put a little more pressure on the knife, and he stepped back away from the blade.

'This is not over.'

He said loudly, trying to salvage something now that he was out of knife range so in my best Eddie Murphy impersonator accent I said,

'You all have a real nice day now Shrek, don't be scaring the children no more.'

That brought some laughter from the rest of the room and he walked off to join PD at his table. Fuck them if they can't take a joke.

The best bit was later that evening walking back from the sheds with one hand on the pistol in my pocket, I saw the Golf GTI on a trailer being taken to the off-site car park for the VW dealers to collect. Ha fucking ha.

I saw Lisa on Wednesday and she wanted all of the details, she made me tell her about the breakfast incident three times. I didn't mention the device that stuffed his car though, kept that one to myself.

25.

Life continued in its very pleasant way until one Saturday a few weeks later. Lisa opened the door and she was wearing a skimpy French Maid / waitress outfit. Wow! Fishnet stockings, white frilly knickers with a short black dress and as she turned to go into the house I could see it was backless, definitely no bra.

'Do you like it?'

'Very much,'

'Good, this was Max's favourite but fuck him. You might as well enjoy it.'

Ah, we were exercising demons now, that was why she had wanted me to finish in her bum on that spectacular Friday. I was currently the last man who had been up there not Max. This was Max's favourite costume and she was now sharing the goodies with me. Result.

She wasn't drunk, just playful, probably a glass of wine but no more.

'If sir would like to come into the dining room, dinner is served.'

Role play. Ok, heard about it, never done it, just go along with the game I suppose. I wonder if she wants me to spank her. Better not ask, better just wait and see.

The dining table was set for two with candles and posh crockery. She showed me where to sit and then served an excellent meal of lobster poached in cream with green beans and a crème brule, which she finished off at the table with a little blowtorch. White wine to drink and I don't think it was the seven quid Naafi one.

'Would sir like coffee in the lounge?'

'Sir would, thank you.'

The coffee was great, out of a proper machine.

She sat next to me and it was very hard to keep my hands off her but I didn't know where we were going with this so I let her take the lead, it was her role play after all.

She had more wine and then said,

'Will sir require service in the bedroom this evening?'

Has any man ever said no? It's a bit like would you like a bacon sandwich? A totally pointless question.

'Yes, sir would like an intimate personal service in the bedroom,'

With that costume and her playfulness, I was surprised that my dick hadn't burst out of my trousers.

'Follow me,'

I don't know if you have ever followed a sexy woman wearing fishnet stockings and frilly knickers up a staircase but I can tell you that it was amazing.

She went into the bedroom and the curtains were shut, with just a candle burning. She turned around and stood in front of me.

'Put your hands behind your head.'

She did. I stepped in close to her, reached under her skirt and pulled her knickers off.

'Sit on the bed please.'

She did.

I stood in front of her and slowly took my clothes off.

'Sir would like you to suck his knob,'

She leaned forward put her hands on my hips and took me into her mouth, it was just as fantastic as I remembered.

I stepped back; I didn't want this to end too soon. I thought I would push my luck and see what happened.

'Sir would like to ride bareback this evening,'

That brought a sharp intake of breath and not from me.

She was struggling with the idea but then she nodded and looked down at the floor. I put my hand under her chin and gently brought her head up so that she was looking at me,

'And sir would like to come inside your pussy.'

Again, the look but she had started the role play, if she had dressed up as a dominatrix she might even now be sticking a large black dildo up my arse. (No, I haven't, but I do know squaddies who have-lol! It's not something I would normally volunteer for but apparently it gives you an amazing orgasm, so if ever Lisa opened the door wearing a PVC cat-suit and a kitten mask then hey-ho!) instead she had chosen the submissive role and so she was going to end the evening with a very wet pussy.

'Spread out on the bed wench,' I said.

Wench, wench where the fuck did I get that from? Still it seemed to work as she lay back on top of the sheets.

'Hands behind your head,'

She did.

'Legs wide open please,'

She did, I was enjoying this,

'Touch your clit with your finger,'

'No,'

'Now,'

She moved her right hand down and with two fingers began to touch herself. I was just about to explode but I wondered how far we could go with this. I was getting the warm musky smell of an aroused woman at this point, something I have always enjoyed. Then her hips started twitching, shit she was really into this.

'Stop' I said,

She moaned softly, then put her hand back behind her head.

She was breathing very heavily and I figured it was time for my entrance. I knelt between her legs and lifted them up just as I had with Laura, I had enjoyed that position so I did the same to Lisa. Pinning her hands by the side of her head and pushing her legs down onto her chest with my weight. She was gasping now as I started thrusting and then it was all over. Wow. I stayed where I was until the twitching had finished and slipped out of her, the sheets were going to need washing anyway so I just sprawled on the bed with my arm around her. I reached for her clit, but she moved my hand away.

After a while she said,

'I enjoyed that,'

'Me too.'

Even if it was more about Max than me, still, never refuse a wet pussy that is my motto. Well it is now.

She went off to the bathroom and I got dressed, she came back in wearing a pink jogging suit which was not as sexy as the costume but you can't have everything. We went and watched some tv then went to bed as normal. (She had changed the duvet cover)

I woke to the smell of sausage this time which was just as welcome, I went down and she was wearing the jogging suit, standing at the cooker. I went up behind her and put my arms around her, turned the cooker off and stripped her, right there in the kitchen. I put her arms around my neck and kissed her, with tongues.

'I want you again,' I said,

'OK,'

We went back up to the bedroom and I just laid her down, spread her legs and slipped my cock into her. Does it count as sloppy seconds if it is yours, I'm not sure? A few minutes gentle thrusting and I came again, that's another duvet cover I thought, still not my problem.

'Your sausage is getting cold,'

'My sausage is perfectly fine thanks,'

Still no smile, tough crowd, but I had done her twice in the last few hours so who was winning now Max?

She was very subdued for the rest of the day but I don't think it was about the sex. I was hoping she was having some feelings for me because I was certainly having some feelings for her. Being an escaped war criminal did restrict my dating choices, but I was looking forward to the next few years with the very fine Ms. Phelan. Yes, Ms Phelan, back to the maiden name, Mrs Carstairs was no more. She didn't even need to divorce him as he was legally deceased so she just had all of her documents changed.

I decided to leave about 3 and she came to the door with me.

'I have to tell you something,' She said.

Oh now I understood, this was a 'Fuck-dump' the lads in the shed had talked about this, women screw your brains out and then dump you on the basis that you will be more docile after sex and won't make a big deal out of it. So be it.

'I'm leaving Hereford, I can't stay here, not with what happened with Max. I'm moving to New Zealand, my sister lives there and she has sponsored me for a visa so I can get a job.'

'That's great Lisa, really, I don't know how you have stood it this long.'

What else could I say, 'hang around here and I will bonk you once a week until one of us gets bored?' No this was a good move for her, completely new start.

'I'm so glad you understand,'

'I think I do, when are you leaving?'

'Thursday,'

She took a deep breath,

'I do owe you an apology though.'

'What for?'

'That first time at the siege it wasn't rape. I tried to convince myself that it was but I hadn't been with anyone since Max and really by the time you got my knickers off I was red hot and ready to go. So don't feel guilty about it.'

I didn't feel guilty but I just said,

'They were strange times.'

'Yes, they were.'

'Can I ask you something?'

'What?'

'Can I have a pair of your knickers as a souvenir, those pink ones you were wearing at the siege?'

'No you can't you big pervert, now go and thank you for everything, you saved my life and the lives of all the others so thank you for that.'

The following Tuesday I got back to the mess and saw a brown military envelope in my pigeon-hole in the mess which was very unusual. I didn't get any military mail as I had been dishonourably discharged from the army and was technically still serving my sentence at the CTC. I took it back to my room, opened it and out fell a pair of sexy pink knickers. Result. I did sniff them of course unfortunately they only smelt of being washed but there on the crotch was a small, hand drawn smiley face. Thank you indeed.

26.

We settled in for the winter and worked hard. I'm not a big fan of the very cold weather so on those days I made a packed lunch in the mess and stayed in the sheds all day. I used the gym for keeping fit and the indoor range for shooting practice so overall the winter wasn't too bad.

Yes, I had volunteered for one survival training course in Norway but I discovered then that I really don't like the severe cold. One bit I did learn was the importance of keeping your feet warm and even now I wear old hiking socks in bed in the winter. Unless I have company of course.

Did I miss Lisa? Yes I did, not just for the sex although I am very shallow. I also missed her smile and her quirky sense of humour. I didn't miss the moodiness but I couldn't really blame her for that, she had been treated very badly by people she should have been able to trust and my one hope was that

Max was miserable in his jungle squat (or wherever he was) and he was missing this amazing woman. I missed watching her get dressed on a Sunday morning.

I remembered that one time she was standing in front of her mirror wearing just her underwear, after the news about Max she had changed her hairstyle to a much shorter cut. She was flicking it about with her brush, and said,

'I look like a boy,'

'Not with that arse you don't.'

That's me being the supportive partner.

She had smiled at that and the room had lit up. So yes I did miss her.

It was one Tuesday in late March when Dougie popped his head out of the office, we had been working on one of his many strokes of genius. The blades often had to use cheap Chinese-made motorcycles in various countries where they were working undercover. Thing is these bikes tend to be fairly fragile and they break down a lot which is not what you want when you are out planning devious, special forces type mischief.

Dougie had realised that a lot of these bikes were copies of old Honda designs, Honda being a very reliable make. Dougie had the idea of replacing all of the Chinese made parts that could not be seen from the outside with genuine Honda replacement parts thus dramatically improving the reliability and usefulness of the bikes.

We had asked for a shedload of old bikes to be shipped back to us and we were currently playing with half-a-dozen of them, uprating the engines, gearboxes, electrics and even the internals of the suspension components. This should improve the performance for the guys but the main priority was that the modifications had to be invisible from the outside, hence the term undercover.

'JB wants you,'

Ok wonder what he wants?

Usual short wait outside his office then in.

'Michael, come in, grab a coffee and have a seat.'

Wow, this was a first. He was rumoured to have the best coffee on the base, made in a machine from real beans, not that stuff where the beans have been through a cats arsehole but very good indeed.

I grabbed a cup, put plenty of milk in, in case I wasn't staying long and sat down.

'There's bad news and there's good news,' He said,

'We lost a guy in Afghan last week, tripped an IED made from an old artillery shell, completely vaporised, Sergeant Ian Naismith.'

Bad news indeed.

'Turns out that he was a great soldier but a bit of a loner, no family, no friends no one at all which means that we have an identity that we can now pass over to you.'

Interesting, I hadn't thought of that but maybe they had just been waiting for the right circumstances?

'You are off the clock in the sheds now I need you to get sorted as I want you running logistics in Batus for the summer. So go and see the people in documents and travel, they will get your signature and photos and we will change all of the identity information over, you are on the 5pm flight out of Brize on Friday, OK?

OK? yes please ok. I thought I was stuck on this base forever and now there was an opportunity to be a different person who no one was looking for, thank you very much.

A few busy days then with the folks in documents and travel. I had to get my uniforms renamed and new military ID card, a passport and a driving licence, on which I apparently had six points for speeding, still mustn't grumble. I had two separate haircuts in one day so that they could have different photos on the documents, clever that.

They had worked their magic and all of my fingerprints and dental records were swapped with the unfortunate Sgt Naismith. I had to give some sample signatures for the bank and was very pleased to see that he had fourteen thousand pounds in his account, it seemed that he had never spent much on himself. His car was a very old Audi that I didn't want so that was to be sold and the money donated to the regiments welfare fund.

This new identity also meant that I would be receiving a salary again as well as all the overseas allowances during my summer at the legendary Batus training area. Batus is the British Army Training Unit Suffield, a massive open country training area near the small town of Suffield in Alberta, Canada. One of the few places where the armoured regiments could train with their main battle tanks.

The plan was that I would go out as an advance party and set up in our own separate accommodation on the camp. Four-man teams would come out for a two-week stint and they would go and play, 'Red Team,' with the tankies, basically trying to sneak up on them. Planting bright yellow 'You're dead!' stickers and small Wizz-bang type explosive devices,(not harmful just a surprise!) on the vehicles and kit. Keeps the tankies on their toes and is great training for the blades. In addition I would also be testing a wide range of new vehicles that would be delivered to our workshop for evaluation and then reporting back to HQ.

Friday afternoon I was dropped off at Brize Norton for my flight to Canada. I always loved travelling through Brize, there was usually a good atmosphere and I enjoyed the anticipation of the travel rather than getting bored by the wait. The big question mark was which aircraft would we be using?

The Tristar is a normal airliner which could lift us to Calgary airport in one hit but we might be going in the venerable 'Hercy-bird,' the Lockheed C130 Hercules. Great aircraft but they could not do the distance in one hit so we would need to land and refuel at Goose Bay, an airbase in Eastern Canada, before finishing the journey.

Fortunately, we won the Tristar and it was on time landing at Calgary in the middle of the night. There was a hotel booked for me so I got my head down and went to collect my hire car the following morning. The guys had booked me a people carrier as I would be collecting and dropping off the teams as they came out. This would be swapped every month firstly because it would need servicing by the company and secondly as a security precaution. No worries.

Turned out to be one of the best postings I had ever been on. Our accommodation was a big tank shed on the outskirts of the base with several portacabins inside. One was an office and store, one was my en-suite living quarters complete with TV and small kitchen and two were separate units for the teams to use when they were not out on the area. The food in the mess hall was great if you like maple syrup and I do.

Basically we worked a ten-day programme. I would drive into Calgary on the Sunday, pick up the team and drive them back to Batus. They would sort themselves out and on Monday night I would drive them out onto the training area and drop them off. I had a range of vehicles in the shed which I could use and which would be ignored by the troops on the ground. Same old story, cover something in bright orange tape and it becomes invisible. I had a satellite phone which I kept on twenty-four seven as did the teams, they would ring Zero and Zero would ring me if anything kicked off.

We only had one incident when a guy slipped in the middle of the night and broke his leg. I went out to collect him and took him to the medical centre, he was flown back to the UK and the rest of the team stayed out.

All being well ten days later I would pick them up in the early hours of Thursday morning when they would come back in, shower and change, then back to Calgary where we all got a couple of days off until I picked the next team up on Sunday. I was able to pay for my hotels, food and petrol on the company credit card, the arrangement being that if I spent over my daily allowance for food and accommodation then the office would simply deduct the excess from my salary. This meant that after the first couple of weekends in Calgary I was able to explore all over the province visiting Banff, Jasper and Edmonton on a regular basis. Brilliant.

When the teams were out I got loads of vehicles to play with on the massive training area from quad bikes and motorcycles to four-wheel drive farm vehicles and some quirky stuff that needs to remain secret.

I would spend a week or two blasting around the area on roads and off-road seeing if they were the kind of vehicle we could use.

This was quite a broad remit as the regiment were up to all kinds of operations everywhere from the very cold parts of the world, to the very hot parts of the world and everywhere in between including jungle and urban environments. I had checklists to complete and then a detailed report to write on each vehicle which I sent back to Hereford every week by email.

The farm vehicles were interesting, designed for a rough working life and minimal maintenance which was just what we needed. I had some ideas about one of the Kawasaki farm trucks, bit like you might see on a golf course or being used by the local council gardeners. The thing is Kawasaki make some very fast motorcycles and I wondered if we could fit a big bike engine into the little truck and turn it into a flying machine.

The secret stuff was interesting but often a bit fragile, most blades treat the throttle as if it is a switch either on or off and go everywhere at maximum speed. I had to be 'recovered' several times from the training area by the local troops when the test vehicle expired, usually in a cloud of steam. As I pride myself on being a very sympathetic driver some of these prototypes would not last very long in the hands of my heavy-footed colleagues.

All good things must come to an end I suppose and we were due to finish the programme in the first week of September. I then got a very welcome email telling me to take three weeks leave and report back on the first of October.

Fantastic. I had saved most of my salary and between us Ian and I had almost twenty thousand pounds in the bank. Time for a holiday. I contacted the office to make the travel arrangements which also had the advantage of them knowing where I was and what I was driving and then it was off to my dream destination of Los Angeles, California.

The travel team had done well, flight into LAX in premium economy, whatever that was? They had sorted me a midsize Ford car and booked a long-term apartment stay in a block just back from the shoreline in Manhattan Beach. This quickly became my new favourite place in the world, glorious beach full of young blonde surfers, great places to eat and what seemed like an endless beachside path for jogging, cycling and walking.

Ian treated me to a fancy modern mountain bike with big chunky tyres, which I was planning to ship back to Hereford at the end of the holiday. One day I rode it north past Venice Beach to Santa Monica. I stood on the end of the pier in Santa Monica by the fairground where Route 66 officially ends. I was drinking a coffee and it was difficult not to get a bit emotional, less than eighteen months ago I had been fighting for my life in the siege and had then been prosecuted for war crimes, after that I thought I was stuck in Hereford for life and now here I was.

The apartment had a small kitchen but apart from making a brew and keeping my beer cold I really couldn't be arsed cooking. I got into the habit in the mornings of wandering down towards the beach and having coffee and a croissant at a small café that had a veranda overlooking the shoreline path and a rather tasty blonde waitress who spoke with a strange accent and was either from Sweden or Wisconsin?

It was day four of my holiday and the third time I had eaten at the café. That was when I saw her. The woman.

Let me put this in context California is full of gorgeous women, L.A. is full of very gorgeous women and this woman was spectacular. She had short blonde hair a stunning figure and what I thought were movie star looks. She was wearing an electric blue bikini made from less material than that used in the average wet wipe, with a soft see through jacket over the top. She had the kind of tits that seem to be filled with helium and moved independently from the rest of her body.

The guys will know what I mean when I say that I stopped breathing. Wow.

She came up onto the veranda and walked up to my table,

'Do you mind if I sit here?'

I nodded; I was incapable of speech. She put the jacket over the back of her chair and sat there in all her glory in front of me. The waitress came up to talk to her and some form of conversation took place, I just don't know what it was. This never happens to me and my first ungracious thought was that she was some form of hooker and my second ungracious thought was how much and for how long and dare I use the company credit card?

'I don't like sitting on my own as men keep hitting on me,'

Well there was my opening for an obvious reply,

'What makes you think I won't hit on you?' I said smiling.

She smiled back, reached out and touched my hand,

'Because you are Sergeant Michael Lewis and you are keeping a very low profile.'

27.

Shit, shit, shit, shit, shit and shit! I looked around for any kind of cameras or people coming to arrest me, I could not see any threats but that does not mean that they weren't there. I had not brought a firearm into the states, my pistol had gone back to Hereford in a Movement Box with all my military kit. I had bought one of Ernie Emerson's CQB knives to take back to the UK with me but that was back in the apartment and no use at all really.

'Please do not worry sergeant,' she said,

'I mean you no harm and anyway you can see that I'm unarmed and I'm not wearing a wire.'

To be fair I could see that both of those statements were true.

'I work for some people who think that you have been very badly treated by the army and your government. You should have been given a medal and a promotion for what you did at the siege not thrown into jail.'

WTF?

'We were very pleased when Major Warner sneaked you out of the jail in the boot of his car. We want you to think about working with us and liaising with the military and security officials in the UK.'

WTF? (2)

Who is this woman? Who does she work for? How does she know all this? How on earth did she find me here? What do they want me to do? And finally, is there any chance of a shag? Fine priorities you may think, but I did say I was shallow.

'There are some people who would really like to meet you, can you come with me now, listen to what we have to say then discuss it with Major Warner when you get back to Hereford. If you don't want to work with us then that's fine but I am sure that there are people in the UK who will want to become involved.'

She did speak fairly formerly, almost as if it was rehearsed or as if she was making me a legal offer and really what did I have to lose? If she and her organisation had wanted to hurt me they would have just done it. Also, I was curious as to who they were and what they wanted and of course she did have great tits.

So we walked off together getting a funny look from my favourite waitress, well you know what she can do if she can't take a joke.

We walked up to the main road and there was a black Lincoln Town car waiting for us, great, I have seen them in the movies but never been in one. We got in the back and it was so dark I could not see out so I have no idea which direction we drove in. After about twenty minutes we entered a big garage and the door closed behind us. Starting to get a bit worried now. Still, I had the cheap phone I had bought at the airport in my pocket and Zero had the number so if anything happened?

I followed Cassie, through a door into a corridor, she had told me her name in the car, it was Cassandra but she preferred the shorter version. She was from San Francisco originally and had studied medicine at university before getting involved with the people in her current job which she did not wish to discuss. She did say that we would have plenty of time to talk if I decided to work with the group but she said it fairly seriously rather than as a come-on. I really think she meant talk.

We stopped outside a door with a number 2 on it and she said,

'We need some security because we are going to reveal an awful lot of information about our group. We have a couple of tests for you, if you choose not to join in then you can leave at any time.'

Again with the formal language, she sounded a bit anxious and I wasn't sure why?

'Room 2, then room 4 and I will see you in room 5 when you are finished before you speak to the director. Please come and work with us, it's important'

Ok.

She opened the door and I went in, crap!

The room was about half the size of the twenty-five-metre range at Hereford, obviously used for shooting as there was a firing point with a waist high table with a pistol on it. There were two young guys in the front of the room one was pointing a video camera at me and the other was pointing a pistol at me. So far so good, but the problem was that down the end of the range there were three Asian looking guys duct taped to chairs and someone had given them a real pasting. Shit.

'So the famous Sergeant Michael Lewis,' The guy with the pistol said,

'You don't look very hard to me.'

I said nothing. I needed to leave this place asap, I seemed to have bumped into a bunch of crazies and at this point I didn't care how great her tits were.

'So arsehole,' pistol man continued.

'This is the test, these three were planning to blow up a shopping mall when they appeared on our radar, they have admitted it and now need to be executed. We will film you shooting them and then if you talk to anyone about us, we release the tape and you get life in prison for murder until we have you killed, capisce?'

Well, Cassie was the carrot and this was the stick. I could understand them wanting a hold over me but surely the fact that they knew who I was should be enough. Still I had better go along with them for now.

I walked over and picked up the pistol. It was a Glock which I was familiar with, I sniffed the barrel and it had been fired recently, slipped the magazine off and pressed the top round in, there was good pressure there so I put it back and it seemed like we were good to go.

'How many rounds in the mag?'

Pistol man was now pointing his gun at my head.

'It's a Glock 17 arsehole, it has seventeen bullets in it and they aren't round. You shoot them or I shoot you.'

He laughed at his own joke.

I cocked the action looked up at the end of the range, fortunately the three guys were unconscious, or already dead. I raised the pistol and shot the left-hand prisoner four times in the chest, tracked right and did the same to the other two. I then lowered the weapon to my side and walked over to pistol guy.

'Nice shooting arsehole,' he said, he had also lowered his pistol after I did and that was when I shot him in his right foot. Straight down, lots of little bones in there and very easily explained when you get to casualty, that was why I didn't shoot him in the knees, or head.

He dropped his pistol and fell down clutching his foot.

I pointed mine at the cameraman and said.

'Put the camera down and sit on the floor.'

He did, I was very pissed off now and turned to pistol man who was screaming about what he was going to do to me. I picked up his Glock and thought, been here before, so I pressed his head to the ground with my pistol barrel until he shut up.

'If you ever point a weapon at me again I will kill you, do you understand?'

He nodded and started whining about a doctor and an ambulance but hey, not my problem.

I pointed my gun back at the camera man,

'Take the tape out of the camera and give it to me,'

He did.

'Give me your lighter,'

'I don't have one,'

'Mate, you stink of weed so you have a lighter, you can give it to me or I can take it from your cold dead hands.' When in America etc.

He gave me his lighter and I went to the table and set fire to the tape, while it was burning I stripped both pistols and put the firing pins and springs in my pocket. I went to the door, looked back at them and said,

'Yawl have a real nice day now,'

It came out a bit like my Eddie Murphy impersonation and I am not sure they got the reference. Still, fuck them if they can't take a joke.

The few brain cells I have that have not been damaged by alcohol and petrol fumes were now starting to kick in. Remember where I worked. I was starting to think that there was more to this than a bunch of racist crazies because Hop-along and his camera-carrying buddy were certainly not capable of cracking the security at Hereford and tracking me to L.A. Might just stay with the programme and see what happens?

I went out into the corridor and found room 4, there was no room three, perhaps the sign had been sent away for painting and everyone else knew where it was.

I knocked and went in, oh dear. There was a serious looking young Chinese woman, (or Japanese, or Korean, sorry, I have not met enough people from the Far East to be aware of the difference) she was sitting behind a desk containing what looked very much like a lie detector. Fuck.

She invited me to sit, put a clip on my finger and a strap around my chest. Then she started to ask me some questions, well young lady in the immortal words of Colonel Nathan R Jessop from 'A Few Good Men,' 'You are fucking with the wrong Marine,'

'I cannot answer that question sir.'

My resistance to interrogation training from the dim and distant past had kicked straight into gear, if they thought I was going to answer questions about the regiment and where I worked then they were very much mistaken.

I gave the same reply to the next ten questions and she became exasperated with me. I thought of telling her to go and speak to the last person who had pissed me off but no, I stayed polite and I even did not think of shagging her so I am clearly growing as a person.

I took the strap and clip off and left the room, we were getting nowhere and I had stuff to do.

Room 5 was upstairs according to the sign so I went up and knocked.

'Come in,' this sounded like Cassie and it was. She was wearing a white lab coat and her name badge said she was a doctor. Room 5 was a medical room.

'Hi, can I take some DNA samples from you, just for our records?'

Well not really, but I suppose I should let her as I wanted to see who the ringmaster was in this circus, I had already met the clowns.

She asked me to sit on the couch and swabbed my mouth, then she took a blood sample, that always makes me laugh because my blood group is B positive which is also my philosophy for life – ha ha.

'Can I have a semen sample?'

What can you say to that, I was almost speechless, almost.

'Yes, but you have to take it yourself.'

She smiled and produced a condom, she started to undo my trousers so I started to undo her lab coat, well fair exchange etc. She took my cock out and slipped the condom on and started stroking me by which time I had got her tits out and they were magnificent. I mean Lisa had nice tits but these were spectacular, full, round and not as heavy as I had expected, well anyway I came, she took the condom and then put her tits away. As you have read this far you will know that I have had some very strange days in my life but this was shaping up to be one of the strangest.

'I'm taking you to meet the Director, please listen to what he has to say, please listen to all of it, there is so much riding on this and we really need the UK to be on board.'

I nodded.

I followed her down the corridor to a big steel door at the end, she pressed a button and looked up at a camera above the door. It buzzed and opened, there was a bit of a hallway and there was a guy standing there. He was middle-aged and a bit fat, didn't look like a hard man to me, looked more like an office manager type. Ok.

'Sergeant Lewis, it's an honour to meet you, I have been waiting for today for a long time,'

We shook hands. Cassie left, was this the guy that was making her nervous, didn't see it myself?

'Even though you have shot one of my men,'

'Yes, well, that was part of the test wasn't it, you probably thought I would shoot him in the head and save you the bother,'

The old grey cells had been ticking and I had realised that sticking that moron with a gun in front of me was the test, not the three guys in the chairs.

He roared with laughter,

'I told them you were sharp, it's a pity we lost the film it would have been hilarious,'

'Except that you filmed the whole thing with a hidden camera, the weed smoking womble was obviously not the main cameraman, now are we going to stop pissing about or shall I just go?'

He stopped smiling, 'A serious man, I like that.'

I don't, 'ernste Manner', serious men, is what they called the men who planned the Holocaust. Dangerous waters these.

'I'm known as Senator Bob, but you can call me Bob.'

'OK Bob shall we talk?'

"Yes, but first would you like a drink, whisky, beer?'

'I would like a nice milky coffee please Bob,'

A couple of minutes later and my suspicions were proved correct when a young woman came into the room with a coffee for me and what looked like a large bourbon for Bob. We were being listened to and probably recorded. So be it. Ears open, gob shut.

We went through to an office type room with some easy chairs around a low table. We sat down and Bob began talking. He talked for almost two hours and it was the strangest shit I have ever heard.

Cassie walked me back down to the car when Bob had finished. I could see why she was nervous; this was serious stuff.

'You are now the thirteenth outsider who knows the full plan,'

Unlucky for some I thought, although I don't believe in superstition or astrology or any of that crap, typical Pisces. But I could see what she meant about serious and why they needed someone intelligent to talk to the UK about it, pity they were stuck with me.

The Town Car took me back to the beach and I wandered off and had a fancy burger and a couple of beers. I didn't sleep well that night; I was thinking that I needed to get back to base with this information asap and I thought of trying to get an earlier flight.

Senator Bob had suggested that I keep things as they were to avoid raising any suspicion but I didn't fancy explaining to Colin why I had pissed about playing sandcastles for another two weeks when the regiment could have been onboard.

Walking down to the café for breakfast I decided that I would ring the travel section later that morning and claim to be unwell and ask them to get me on the first plane back. As I reached the corner of the street that led down to the beach I saw a young woman in jogging clothes struggling with a paper map, she was making a right mess of it.

'Excuse me sir, can you show me where I am on this map?'

'I will try,' I said, I am usually pretty good with maps.

I swear I didn't see the stun gun until it was far too late and she jabbed me in the ribs and fired it. Fuck! It was like being kicked by a horse that was plugged into the mains, if you can imagine that. A van pulled up behind me and she pushed me into the open door, a couple of guys grabbed me and put a hood over my head. Then I felt a needle in my thigh and I was truly and right royally fucked.

28.

I woke up when the ice water hit me, shit. I felt awful and even worse when I realised that I was naked and tied to a heavy metal chair. Now if this had been one of Lisa's role-playing games then maybe I would have enjoyed it but the people I saw when I blinked my eyes open were clearly not playing games.

The woman with the map who shall henceforth be known as the bitch or TB was facing me and stabbed me again with the stun gun, fuck that hurt. The guy with her was a fitness freak steroid-user type who shall henceforth be known as Dipstick. He swung a big roundhouse punch at my head and although I tried to ride it I was limited by being tied to the chair and I ended up spitting bits of blood and teeth. TB then shocked me again, shit I thought ask me a fucking question. She did.

'What did they tell you?'

'What is their plan?'

'When is it going to happen?'

She then shocked me again and Dipstick hit me with his other fist right in the stomach and I brought the burger and the two beers right back up onto my lap. Fuck me this is awful.

I assumed they were talking about Cassie and Senator Bob and that I was going to be in a world of hurt if I didn't talk but then two thoughts occurred to me, one, was that I needed to zone out as I did when life got too shitty and two, what if this was part of the test?

Was Senator Bob setting me up? Beat the crap out of me but if I talk and reveal their plans then I would just get a bullet in the head because they would not be able to trust me. Bit like the interrogation training that the blades do, where whatever they do to you, you know it's actually a barn near Hereford and you are not going to be killed. (not really though)

'Fucking answer me.' TB screamed in my face.

'I cannot answer that question sir,'

'We know you are a Brit; we don't think Naismith is your name and we know you have military ID. You met with some dangerous people yesterday and we want to know what they told you.'

'I cannot answer that question sir,'

She zapped me again, I think either the battery was running down or I was getting used to it but it did not feel as bad that time.

Dipstick punched me in the face again and even though I twisted my head I still lost a few more teeth.

She screamed at me a bit more,

'I cannot answer that question sir,'

Then he came around to the side and kicked my chair over, I tried to shield my head but it still hit the ground hard and I lost consciousness for a second or two.

'You need to think about this whoever the fuck you are, we can rendition your arse to Gitmo and you will just disappear.'

Aha, a clue. They walked over to a door in the corner of the room and left me lying on the ground, crap I have had better days. But the clue was in the Gitmo reference, these were probably Homeland Security or CIA. I hope that the FBI would have been a little more professional but whoever they were I was in the shit.

Unless the Gitmo reference was part of Senator Bob's cunning plan and I was meant to tell all to these charming representatives of American Law Enforcement and then they would shoot me in the head. I had heard of Catch 22 but had never been in it until now. It wasn't very pleasant.

I looked around and saw that I was in a big storeroom with windows high up in the walls, there had been a funny smell when they opened the door but I could not remember what it was, there was not much noise coming in from outside so I had no clue where I was. Well I did I suppose, I was lying on a concrete floor tied to a metal chair but that was not much help.

They came back in after a while, there was more kicking, screaming and zapping with the stun gun and lots more of,

'I cannot answer that question sir,'

Then after a while they almost seemed to get tired of hurting me and left me lying on the floor, alone.

I passed out at various times during the night although you would not call it sleep. I woke up when I got the ice water treatment again, desperately trying to get some in my mouth only to find they had put salt in it. Fuck.

The second day was a repeat of the first with me getting hurt and them getting nowhere. I was truly fucked, if I talked I would die, if I didn't I would suffer. They seemed to be getting weary of the process and kept going into the corner to have little chats, once she got a phone call and I think she was telling someone that I was a stubborn son of a bitch but they would break me soon.

I then seemed to be getting a bit delirious, I kept thinking I was back in the siege, then at the Court-Martial, then in Lisa's bedroom, then was very disappointed to find that I was not in Lisa's bedroom. I kept seeing people I had served with who had been killed, a village in Afghan after an air strike, camel spiders in Iraq and scenes from my childhood, none of which were very pleasant.

They had to keep throwing the ice water at me so they could zap me and hit me again, I then started mumbling about the past but I am sure that I was making no sense at all.

They left me on the floor for the second night and I was pretty sure that I was going to die and bizarrely it didn't seem to matter anymore. I was drifting in and out of consciousness and having flashbacks to other scary moments from my life and my military service. Then I must have passed out completely.

On the third day they hit me with the ice water, a couple of zaps with the gun but that did not bother me as much now, I had moved into some sort of zone where I was out of it. I had stopped talking as that seemed to be the safest option and just sat there whatever they did.

TB got a phone call and was swearing at the person on the other end, she was not happy with what she had been told and was asking for one more day. The person she was speaking to was very insistent and seemed to be giving her orders.

She walked back to where Dipstick was standing and said,

'Shit, they have pulled the plug, we have to take him back,'

'What, we have to take him back?'

'Yes on the plane all the way, fuck, we could have broken him today'

I was largely out of it at this stage and it could all have been a wind up anyway. They used all sorts of tricks on the blades when they were training, there was some old bloke dressed as a workman who would come into the interrogation room when they had been starving for a week.

The old man would say he was just getting his lunch and offer them half of a bacon sandwich. Take the butty and you fail the course, so I wasn't getting excited about something that might not happen.

Dipstick took a knife out of his pocket and sliced the ropes holding me to the seat, I was lying on the floor and as I stretched my limbs out I was in agony. He went to the wall and took a hose pipe and fired it at me, even that hurt but as I had shit myself whilst on the chair I could see his point, I managed to get some of the water in my mouth. Result.

TB came back into the room and threw some orange overalls at me. Been there done that I thought. I painfully put them on and then tried to stand, I rolled onto my knees and crawled after them to the door.

TB said, 'We have to take you back but we will be watching you,'

Watch away I thought, you will get bored before I do and next time show up without the stun gun and see what happens bitch.

I managed to get to my feet and stumbled out of the door after them, turned out we were in a big hangar and there was one of those executive jets you see millionaires flying around in Fuck! That was the smell I could not place, aviation fuel. They put handcuffs on me, in front of me and dragged me to the plane, up the steps and then dumped me in the first pair of seats nearest the door. They went up to the front of the plane and sat down.

The aircrew was a young marine who took one look at me and fetched me a bottle of water, I managed to start drinking some and TB yelled,

'Don't give that scumbag anything.'

'This is my aircraft ma'am and this man is hurt, if you don't like it I suggest that you get the fuck off my plane or shut the fuck up.'

Oh perfect, she was definitely fucking with the wrong marine.

The plane took off and we flew into the darkening sky. I was not sure what day it was or where we were going, it could have been an economy flight to Gitmo. The marine was a hero, after the water he brought me some yoghurt having seen the state of my teeth, then he made some coffee, I have never tasted coffee as good as that was. I noticed that he didn't make any for TB and Dipstick.

Maybe it was the circumstances, maybe it was just good coffee but I started to feel a little more human. I hadn't noticed but my bare feet were bleeding, he put some plastic gloves on, bathed them with antiseptic, dried them with some paper towels and then gave me some slippers like you see in airline adverts for first class passengers. Then I fell asleep.

It transpired that what had saved me was the credit card. HQ had noticed that I spent something on it every day, I had not used it on the morning I was grabbed so after two days in LA with no purchases they had started making enquiries.

The story went that some high-up person in Homeland Security had a massive horse ranch. He was being difficult about my detention until someone from the regiment asked him if he had seen the Godfather. Bearing in mind who was asking him the question, he had rung TB immediately and that was the call I had overheard. Result.

29.

The plane touched down gently in the middle of the night. I had heard that there was an 'unofficial' airstrip near the camp that was used for clandestine comings and goings, but I had never been there.

They dragged me to the top of the steps and I could see Colin leaning on his Jag at the edge of the strip. The male agent dragged me down the stairs holding my handcuffs and the Bitch followed closely behind. Apparently, they had been told to hand me over in person to someone from the UK.

We stopped at the bottom of the steps and I turned to face the aircraft whilst Dipstick undid the cuffs, they had their backs to the plane and as I looked up I said,

'Is that a fire?'

They would have been superhuman not to have glanced back at the plane. They were not superhuman and that gave me the second that I needed.

Some people will tell you that a punch starts in the hip, thrusting forward providing momentum for the arm to channel the power into the fist. My old Shotokan instructor insisted that a good punch starts in the heel. This one did, starting in the heel of my standing foot, driving up through my hip and onwards into my fist.

As Dipstick turned back towards me my fist connected with his face just under his nose and I aimed for the back of his head. Most people punch someone in the face and stop; I followed through with 12 stones of very angry vehicle specialist behind it. He went down, no choice really I think he was unconscious before he hit the floor, however, as he went down and before he hit the floor I had grabbed the pistol from his shoulder holster and smacked the Bitch in the face with it hard, caught her just under the eye and I felt her cheekbone smash.

She went down like someone who had been struck in the face with a lump of metal, appropriate really and by the time she had hit the floor I had cocked the pistol and shot him once in each knee. Painful and very inconvenient but not life threatening, I tracked the pistol slightly to my left and shot her in each knee as well.

'Sir, sir,' the marine was shouting from the top of the aircraft steps, he was holding a shotgun which he must have grabbed from just inside the door.

'Put the weapon down – now!'

I looked down at the two assholes who had tortured me for three days and smiled,

'Look at your chest Marine,'

I advised him and when I looked up, I saw as he did the 4 laser targeting dots on his chest. I could not see the snipers but I did not expect to, Colin Warner from the regiment at a disused airfield in the middle of the night, no way he was not covered.

Just then Tina appeared and as always, she was a game changer. You may have seen pictures on the news of 'technicals' usually in some god-forsaken war zone populated by the AWF (arseholes with firearms). Usually based on a Toyota pick-up they are modified with some heavy weapons and become a sort of ad hoc military vehicle.

We had taken this a step further and mounted an M61 6-barrel anti-aircraft cannon on the back of our Toyota pickup but the secret was that we had heavily modified the original hybrid technology which meant that Tina could run silently on battery power. Appearing out of the mist she had the capacity to completely destroy the aircraft and everyone on board.

She was named after a young lady of the town who had been very attractive, had a thing for troopers and had gone through the regiment like a dose of salts, or more accurately like a dose of chlamydia and sundry other sexually transmitted diseases. Tina in her time, did more damage to the regiment than Saddam Hussein.

The marine acted quickly putting the shotgun back into the aircraft he ran down the steps and lifted the Bitch in his arms, he stumbled back up the steps with her and a second or two later he reappeared with some guy in a pilots uniform and together they lifted Dipstick off the ground and as they dragged him up the steps the marine said;

' Sir, I need that weapon back,'

'No chance,' I replied,

' Spoils of war'.

I knew that dipstick would be in the shit for losing his pistol as well as in the hospital having his knees reassembled - fuck him, because I definitely can't take a joke.

He came back to the door opening and started to close up the steps,

'Marine' I yelled, he looked back at me,

'Thank you for your kindness sir.'

He looked at me and nodded.

The plane door closed and the engines spooled up as it wound up for take-off. I think they call it a tactical withdrawal but, in the event, it was very wise.

I limped slowly over to where Colin was standing,

'Bad day?' he asked,

'Bad three days, ' I said. Then loudly I said,

'Colin you old bastard, how are you?'

And grabbed him in a bear hug. Now this guy was the Ops officer for a very serious bunch of people and there was no way I would ever call him anything but 'Boss, Major or sir' depending on who else was around, he also was definitely not a hugger. Using the hug, I swung him away from the Jag and whispered,

'Your cars bugged'

He tensed for a second and then said loudly,

'I am fine you wanker, much better than you, even if you forgot rule one!'

'What's rule one?'

'Shoot the women first, always.'

'I'll remember that, thanks.'

He slapped me on the back and then helped me into his car. Tina the Technical had vanished into the mist and I wondered how close we had come to having a mangled American jet burned out in a field near Hereford?

I rode in the front seat of the Jag which was a treat for me. Colin looked at me and indicated his eyes, I shook my head and pointed to my ears, sound only, he nodded. In my long chat with Senator Bob he had told me stuff he could only have heard from Colin's car, but I was fairly sure that they only had audio.

'I need to talk to you, boss, as soon as possible, I met some amazing people in America, they want to work with us, going forward'

'Yea, we will get in the SCIF as soon as the medics clear you.'

The SCIF was a safe room in the HQ block which was proofed against any kind of eavesdropping device.

It was where they planned the darkest stuff that never came out in the memoirs because it never happened, a bit like my release from custody if you know what I mean.

We reached the edge of the field and the Range Rover chase car tucked in behind us. This was occupied by four heavily armed members of the CRW, (Counter Revolutionary Warfare) duty team who would splat any vehicle or person who tried to hold us up. I just hoped there were no drunk drivers about tonight as the consequences of even a low speed shunt with the Jag would be catastrophic.

Let me give you an example, you know the wildlife documentaries when you see the mama grizzly bear with her cubs? Well you would have more chance poking her with a sharp stick than getting in the way of our little convoy tonight.

'Double D is waiting up for us, need to get you checked out.'

Double D was one of the doctors on the base, she was different from most military doctors in that she was friendly and really seemed to care about her patients. Most army doctors think that you find sympathy in the dictionary between shit and syphilis, but she was a star. She was an attractive woman in her thirties, but she was even more attractive because she was such a caring doctor.

Her husband was some big shot surgeon who worked in London during the week and the general opinion was that he was a fool for leaving this gorgeous woman to sleep on her own whilst he was away. And no, Double D was not her bra size, she was DD the Deputy Doc. The Big D, the Colonel in charge of the medics, was her boss and in his case his nickname of 'Big D' was based on his being a Dickhead

Colin was talking to Zero the base comms on his hands free, asking for Tango Foxtrot to meet us at the med centre. The unit dentist was a big rugby playing South African with fingers like sausages but there was no way that the SAS dentist was ever going to be called anything but the tooth fairy!

We swept through the camp gates without slowing down and went straight to the med centre. Double D came out to the car and put a neck brace on me, an orderly helped me into a wheelchair and they gave me a gas canister to suck on, it tasted a bit metallic but seemed to take the edge off the pain.

Colin came around to where I was sitting and said,

'We need to debrief as soon as,'

I nodded, ouch.

'Not tonight,' Double D said, 'and probably not tomorrow night either,'

'Its important Doc,'

'Yes, Major, it always is but he is mine now so you can go and practise your mayhem somewhere else and as soon as he is fit you can have him back.'

He grinned, 'Yes, doctor,' and left us to it.

The next hour was a blur of pain and suffering. They cut my jumpsuit off and sorted the burns out. Stuck me through the MRI and then the x ray machine, (good healthcare at Hereford) then the tooth fairy stuck his massive fingers in my mouth, pulled out the remaining bits of teeth and swabbed the damaged gums with some thick smelly stuff, to be fair the pain in my mouth died down a bit so that was ok with me.

Finally, Double D told me that I had a concussion from my head smacking on the concrete, a cracked jaw, numerous broken ribs and some fairly nasty electrical burns, I could have told her that but did not wish to seem ungrateful. Antibiotics, rehydration, painkillers and rest were what I needed.

'Thanks Doc but I do need to speak with Major Warner as soon as possible,'

'OK but tonight you sleep in the med centre and I will review you in the morning.'

She gave me a handful of pills and some water, I swallowed them all and don't remember much after that.

I slept in the sick bay in a private room, I was on a drip for the antibiotics and rehydration but fortunately I could manage the toilet myself. Double D checked on me every day after my blood results had come back but whilst I had been fairly fit prior to the torture the inflammation was not dropping as fast as she would have liked. On day three I asked her about the possibility of me linking up with Major Warner.

'If I can't control the infection on these burns then we may have to amputate the burnt bits including your penis.' She said, 'So just how urgent is this chat with Major W?'

'Not urgent at all Doctor please take your time,'

She smiled at that.

So pain, drips and boredom, there was a TV in the room but have you seen daytime TV? The show 'Loose Women' was not at all what I was expecting, at least I could enjoy the property shows.

On day four I was lying naked on the bed as she was spraying my burns with antiseptic. This happened every day and I had become used to the experience. She looked at me and said,

'I am asking this as your doctor in complete confidence. Do you have sex with men or women?'

Well. I wondered where this was going.

'Women, only women.'

'Good,' she said, she stepped back and undid the top three buttons of her white coat, she was wearing a light blue bra with white lace edging and she had really nice tits. She pushed them in with her hands emphasising her cleavage.

'What do you think of these then?'

What could I do, I got an erection.

Guys, I don't know if you have ever had a burn on your dick which has scabbed over and you have then got an erection and broken the scab but shit that was painful. She sprayed my dick with antiseptic and buttoned her coat up.

'That's good.' She said, 'I was worried that there might be some nerve damage but it looks like you are ok.'

What could I say, she draped a towel across my waist but it was still sticking up like a flagpole.

'I need you to check your sperm for me every time you ejaculate, there may be a little blood in it for the first couple of times and that's no problem, if you still get blood in it after a couple of weeks you need to come in and see me again.'

I could have made a rude comment then but she was so nice and so serious that I just agreed to keep her up to date on all developments in that area.

On day five I came off the drip and she agreed that I could meet with Colin. An appointment was made at the SCIF for 2.30. One of the orderlies wheeled me over in a wheelchair but did not come into the room with us.

30.

'So Michael, been in the wars again?'

'Yes boss,'

'So what the fuck happened in the US?'

I gave him the highlights and he told me that they had found the bug in his car but decided to leave it for now. One update he gave me was that the plane had flown TB and Dipstick out to Ramstein air force base in Germany for treatment. The regiment had sent someone in to slot them but it had already been done. They had both been overdosed with insulin and were now thoroughly deceased. Result, although I was hoping to have the opportunity of sticking her stun gun right up her arse before pulling the trigger.

'So tell me what happened with this Senator then?'

'He is part of a group called TAB, which stands for 'Taking America Back.'

Their plan works on two levels; taking America back to the glory days when everyone had jobs, it was a land of opportunity, good education and the healthcare was the best in the world. But they are also taking America back from the criminals, the corrupt bankers, lawyers and big corporations that are dragging the country down. They call themselves the 'Re-Founding Fathers' and they are going to take control of America.'

'Is this for real?'

'Boss they have bugged your car and just slotted two dickheads on a heavily guarded US air force base. As far as I can tell they are for real.'

He nodded, 'So what's their plan then?'

'They are going to bring all of the US military forces back into the continental US. Alaska and Hawaii are going to keep their garrisons but they are going to concentrate on the mainland. With the reserves and national guard you are looking at,'

'Almost two million troops?'

'Yes.'

'Shit,'

'Yes,'

'They are going to repeal the Posse Comitatus Act and re-interpret the American Constitution. They claim that the original meaning has been lost and that they have the true direction for the USA.'

'What about Afghan are they just going to leave it?'

I took a deep breath and looked down at the floor.

'No, they are going to wipe it off the face of the earth.'

'The whole country?'

'Yes, they have been buying old Russian nukes on the black market, refurbishing them with modern triggers and burying them in new construction projects right throughout the country and up the Swat valley into Pakistan.'

'That will kill millions of people.'

'Yes, he did use the expression, 'serious men','

'How are they going to fire them?'

'They have set up a dummy company in Southern Kazakhstan which is manufacturing space rockets, on 'Future-Freedom Day' or FFD as they are calling it, they will fire rockets into Afghanistan and then blow the nukes so it will look like an attack by

Russia. The estimate is that the whole country and the border region will be uninhabitable for a hundred years. As soon as the rockets are fired the US will go to Defcon One, with all of their missiles pointed at China and Russia.'

'Right, we need a break, I have to go and brief the boss on this. Do you want a coffee when I come back in?'

'Yes please sir, milk no sugar.'

'Roger that.'

And he left.

He was gone about twenty minutes and then he came back in with the Colonel and a woman major from the Intelligence Corps who I hadn't met before. They were all looking very serious. He had forgotten my coffee but never mind.

'So Michael everyone is up to speed so far, now tell us more about this TAB organisation.'

'They have a manifesto' I said, 'alphabetised so it's easy to remember,

A, is for America First, which is their guiding principle.

B, is for Borders, they are going to secure them with the military, with minefields on land and the navy working with the coastguard to search ships coming in. On FFD they will make them all one-way only, people can leave but not come in. Undocumented people will be given twenty-eight days to leave after that they will be jailed or deported to their country of origin. No immigration or tourism will be allowed during the first phase of the operation.'

I was trying to use as much of Bob's language as I could remember rather than put my own spin on it and maybe get something wrong.

'C, is for the currency; they are changing it over to New Dollars which will be red not green. All of the cash that is stashed illegally will be worthless, people will only be able to swap the old stuff for New Dollars if they can prove that they own it legally. All dollars held in foreign banks will be worthless.

D, is for drugs, they are making all drugs legal and they will be supplied by pharmaceutical companies, with the same restrictions that alcohol has. Also they are going to destroy the criminal drug gangs.'

Colin chipped in,

'They are some of the most violent gangs in the world,'

'Yes sir but they will send SEAL teams and Delta after them, there will be a fifty per cent death rate in the gangs,'

'What if they surrender first?'

I took a deep breath.

'There will still be a fifty per cent death rate, these are serious people,'

'Shit,' said the Colonel,

Shit indeed sir. I continued,

'E, is for Equality and Education. Because they are talking about America First then black people and poor people are going to get a much better deal. Schools, housing and opportunity will all be improved. They are going to disarm the police forces so that they only have non-lethal weapons, they will have military back-up for extreme situations but black people won't be killed in routine traffic stops anymore.

The schools will all have at least two armed military personnel, either serving or retired, on the staff. The days of school shootings will be over because any nutcase turning up with a gun will be shot dead, dead not injured, that will be the policy.

All further and higher education will be free and students will be selected on merit, not money and who their family is. That way the country's brightest and best will get the best education, ready for the future.

F, is for Family Finance; every citizen will receive a standard minimum income when they leave school. Enough money for food, accommodation and education. If they choose to work then that is extra money for them, they still get the minimum payments. They are going to try and wipe out poverty

G, is for Guns; they are going to stop people owning them, ban gun shows and close gun stores.'

The intelligence major jumped in here,

'The gun lobby will never allow that.'

'They have thought of that ma'am. Firstly, they are going to stop selling guns and ammunition so eventually the gun nuts will run out. Secondly, they will not be influenced by the political clout of the current gun lobby as they will be independent of any outside influence, either from big business or the NRA because they are not seeking re-election. Thirdly, all the 'Open Carry' stuff will be abolished, if you walk down a street with a firearm you will go to jail the same day, that's if you have not been shot dead by the military. And finally, in what I personally think is a stroke of genius they are going to

Federalise the militias and bring them onside to use against the drug gangs.'

'Fuck,' she said, then looked at the Colonel, 'Sorry sir,'

'No need to apologise Maddy, fuck sounds about right,' He said.

'Go on sergeant,'

'H, is for Health; they have a great health service at the moment if you can pay for it but they are going to change that to something more like our NHS where people are treated by what they need rather than by what they can pay. The big health companies will be abolished and there will be a national system run by doctors with a minimum of administration.

Clinics will be drop-ins with no appointments needed and on-site pharmacies for the minor stuff.

Hospitals will still do the complex stuff but all of the Hollywood style nonsense, plastic surgery and breast enlargements will stop, the doctors will only work on people who are actually sick.

I, is for Independence; they will still celebrate Independence Day because that was when they beat us but they are also going to make America independent of the rest of the world and self-sufficient in everything they need. In the first phase they will stop trading with the rest of the world and cancel all foreign investment in the US. All overseas aid will stop and the United Nations will be invited to relocate to another country. They will not be the world's policeman anymore.

Everything they need they will produce in the US, that will boost the economy and job opportunities for citizens. They may need smaller cars so that they will be self-sufficient with fuel but they will make those cars in the US. There will be less driving and no commercial planes flying so pollution will reduce. They describe it as a win-win.

Young people will do public service, called the Freedom Volunteer Program, from the age of seventeen to twenty, this will be a great programme giving them the opportunity to support their own communities or to travel inside the US and support others or to join the military if they wish. They will build houses and infrastructure, get qualifications in practical skills and broaden their horizons.

J, is for juries and jails. The power that lawyers currently have will be gone, there will be far fewer miscarriages of justice because the FBI will supervise the police forces and the judicial systems. Their financial crimes people will have massive powers to tackle big business and any financial corruption that they discover. If a company tries to rip people off then the directors and senior officers will be put in jail the same day, whilst the investigation takes place.

Citizens will get a fairer trial and the courts and judges will be expanded so that they have time to manage cases properly.'

'What about jails?' Colin asked.

'Jails will be run by the military, there will initially be a massive expansion in capacity using shipping containers. That will be until people get the message. There will be no jail gangs anymore because prisoners will be put in a cell which will have a shower and a toilet and there they will stay 24/7, in the cell. There will be no mobile phone service anywhere and any prison staff found bringing contraband in will be put straight into a cell. There will also be a confidential helpline for any staff who are threatened on the outside with a swift and violent response available from the military.

So you can see the effect this will have on the white-collar criminals who won't be able to hide behind their lawyers and their money anymore.

K, is for the Klan and all the other extremist groups. They will be banned. Simple as.

L, is for language, everyone will be required to speak American no matter what their heritage, if they don't speak American then they don't get the minimum payments.

And that was as far as we got in the two hours I had with Senator Bob; my head was spinning when I left but I have tried to remember as much as I could.'

They didn't speak for a few minutes; they were as stunned as I had been.

'What do they want from us?' The Colonel said,

'Sir, the regiment has a reputation for doing what needs doing and keeping very quiet about it. If they approached politicians with this it would be on the TV news the same day. They want us on board because after phase one they are only going to deal with English-speaking countries, us and Canada. They also want us to keep an eye on Europe for them.'

We all left the SCIF and I was wheeled back to the sick bay

31.

On day six my blood results were better and Double D sent me back to the mess on condition that I came into the med centre every day to talk to Doctor J. Dr. J. is the regiments PTSD specialist, the regiment having learned to take that condition very seriously over the past few years. I had no problem with that and Double D made it clear that both she and Dr. J. would have to sign me off as fit before I could return to duty.

It was great to get back to my own room especially as I was now allowed to drink. My teeth were still a mess but the tooth fairy was prepping me for implants and had put some temporary teeth in which would be ok if I was careful about what I ate.

As instructed I wandered up to the med centre at 10.45 the following day for my 11am appointment with Dr. J. She turned out to be a pleasant middle-aged woman with a soft voice. She settled me into a chair in her office and we just sat there, saying nothing.

'So how does this work then Doctor?'

'Exactly as it is doing.'

So we sat there, fair enough.

The clock went round to 11.50 and she said,

'Same time tomorrow please.'

Fair enough, I thought I can hack this.

The following day was the same, fifty minutes of pleasant silence and,

'Same time tomorrow please.'

I showed up again thinking this would be a doddle, I was wrong because halfway through the session I got the shakes and they were bad. I have never done that in front of any other living person ever. At one point I wondered if I were having some sort of seizure but she just sat there as calm as you like whilst I twitched about in the seat. Then I fell asleep.

I woke up feeling like crap and looked at the wall clock to see that it was just after 4pm, I had slept for about five hours. There must have been a camera somewhere because after a couple of minutes Dr. J.

came into the room and asked me if I was feeling better.

'Not right now,' I said,

'You will,' she said, 'See you tomorrow.'

I drank some stuff that night. I had heard some whispers in the mess that PTSD was a bastard and that the treatment made you feel worse before it made you feel better. When I woke up I felt dreadful but that was probably the half-bottle of gin I had drunk masking the PTSD symptoms.

I was getting to like porridge for breakfast but I was also dying for a slice of fried bread, army fried bread is the best I have ever tasted but with the state of my teeth I would have to wait. Then I had a slow wander up to the med centre using a stick in my right hand. I was still getting a lot of pain in my hip.

Double D thought I had been injured by being dragged about whilst I was unconscious or else by trying to stop my head hitting the floor when the chair had been kicked over. We didn't know what it was, the joint was ok and the physio had given me some exercises so we were just hoping it would get better.

Dr. J. welcomed me into her room and then we talked, it was as if yesterday's attack had broken the spell. Over the next couple of weeks we talked about the torture, the siege, my army service in some of the worlds shittiest places, then inevitably my childhood which I had never talked to anyone about and then how I felt about all of the people I had killed – heavy stuff.

She then did something with my eye movements but I was not sure how effective that was. After a couple of weeks I didn't feel as desperate as I had been doing so I was hoping that something was working.

In the meantime I had been pottering about the camp as Double D thought it would do me good. I had gone down to the sheds and found that everything had changed. Dougie had gone on promotion to the training depot and two of the other guys had gone to Finland on an operation. The only one left that I knew was Alfie and he was living back on the camp as Sheila had kicked him out. Something to do with a woman he had met on his stag do. Too much drama for me and they were very busy so I left them to it.

Fortunately, Charlie was still in the armoury and I spent many happy afternoons down there chatting and helping him with the smaller weapons which I could work on sitting down. He brought me up to date. PD and Shrek had gone, posted to a TA unit in Leeds which was apparently a bit of a downgrade without anyone acknowledging that it was. NTA had got the

RSM's job which meant that the whole camp seemed to have calmed down a bit and was running much more effectively.

Three weeks later Colin called me in, sat me in his office and gave me some good coffee and some good news.

'Michael, you may be aware that sometimes troops from here are seconded to foreign governments and are off the books for a while.'

I had heard bits about this and wondered if that is what Max is doing.

'We have a system for managing the payments they get and also any bonuses.'

He told me that they had an arrangement with the tax people and whatever came in the tax people took twenty per cent off the top then asked no further questions. The regiment welfare fund took half of what was left and the squaddie got the rest, basically forty percent of the money. This was handled by the bank we all banked with in a 'shadow' account which could be accessed without the soldier having any problems of accounting for where the money came from.

'The US government has paid you one million dollars as compensation for the treatment you received, turns out they were Homeland Security and allegedly it was not authorised.'

'So I get?'

'Four hundred thousand dollars, just over three hundred thousand pounds.'

Wow! That sounds like a lot.

'Couple of points, you need to be sensible with this money, if you turn up at a Lamborghini garage the bank will ring here and will not authorise the payment. Most guys buy a house where they plan to live when they leave the army and rent it out to cover the costs until they are ready to use it. That way the money keeps growing. There are people in the admin office who can help you sort it out.'

'A lot to think about sir.'

'Indeed, it's in your account now so enjoy it but don't enjoy it too much.'

32.

Five weeks later, I was still wandering about limping a little and seeing Dr. J. once a week. I came back into my room and saw a white envelope sitting on my drinks tray addressed to 'Sgt Michael Lewis.' I opened it and thought oh fuck!

On the back I wrote, SCIF-PLEASE-URGENT, in big letters and went over to the HQ building. IQ2 was Colins new aide, another stunning blonde who was also as miserable as f**k, where did he find these women? She was sitting in front of Colin's office and I showed her the message. She may have been stuck-up and miserable but she was not working here because she was daft. She did not speak just typed into her computer, after a couple of minutes she got a reply, wrote 12.30 on a post-it note and showed it to me. I mouthed 'thank you' and went back to the mess for lunch.

At 12.15 Colin was standing outside the SCIF looking puzzled, we went in and I handed him the envelope.

'Found this in my room this morning.'

He looked at the contents and said,

'Fuck.'

In his hand was a first-class air ticket in my Ian Naismith identity, from London to Billings, Montana for this Saturday. TAB wanted me in the US.

He thought for a while, I could see that he was shocked that they were inside the base.

'I cannot order you to go, you are not badged to the regiment, you are not trained for undercover or covert work, there is no way you can take any kind of comms gear and we cannot support you. These people are too well organised for that.'

He thought for another few minutes, this was scary, this is a guy who always knows what to do, he was someone you would follow into action in a heartbeat and he was struggling.

'If they ever suspect that you are not onside they will kill you and leave your body in a ditch. No-one would ever blame you for staying here, you have done enough for this country, you could work here in the sheds then retire to the seaside and live very well. This is likely to be a suicide mission. The problem is I really need you to go.

We have war-gamed this scenario, Russia will smash into Europe, China and North Korea will splat Japan and take over the whole of the far east including Taiwan. India and China will square up at the border and India and Pakistan will fire nukes at each other. Iran and Iraq will destroy Israel and then move onto Saudi turning off the world's supply of oil, causing an economic meltdown. ISIS and the other groups will run riot through the chaos taking the world back a thousand years.

The estimate is that without the balance that America provides, over one billion people will die in the first wave of conflicts and the rest of the world will be back in the dark ages.'

'So do you want me to go and disrupt them completely or are we going to be onboard with some of the changes they want to make to America?'

I had to ask because some of what TAB were talking about seemed to make sense to me. Better provision for poor people, sorting out the drug gangs and the financial crimes people.

'I need you to fuck them and their horses and anyone they have ever met.'

'Fair enough sir, I will send you a postcard from Montana.'

He nodded.

I spent a few days sorting the minimum amount of stuff that I could take with me and two days later one of the mess staff handed me a note saying 'SCIF-1500'.

OK. I went along expecting to see Colin but instead I saw a young woman wearing jeans and a jumper holding two big art pads and some pens standing outside, we went in and she handed me a pad and a pen. Therapy, I thought? No, she held up her pad and it had,

JULIA-GCHQ, written on,

Wow, we were in the SCIF and still not speaking, this was getting more serious every day, if they could listen in on the SCIF we were really in trouble.

Basically, Julia was a computer person from GCHQ. She wanted to establish some communications that I could use if I ever got access to the TAB computer network. If I could send her a link then they could mine all of the data from the network and be in a position to stop what was happening. Like the destruction of an entire country.

The link had to be a minimum of sixty numbers which GCHQ could scan for, it had to contain a distress code, something that would indicate if I was compromised and be easy enough for me to remember without writing it down.

I thought for a few minutes, drew the old phone buttons on my pad, where 1 is ABC etc, and wrote out the numbers, I inserted 0 as a spacer between each word with the proviso that a genuine message would not have the 0 between the final two words.

Julia wrote it down then took my copy and asked me to repeat it. I did and she was happy. She thought for a minute and then wrote,

YOU NEED TO UNDERSTAND THAT IF WE GET THE MESSAGE WITH THE DISTRESS CODE, THEN WE MAY HAVE TO TRIGGER A MISSILE STRIKE ONTO YOUR LOCATION?

I nodded; I would be in deep shit anyway so that might be a useful exit strategy.

Early on Saturday morning I was outside the mess waiting for my transport when Colin pulled up in the Jag.

'Michael, just wanted to wish you well,'

'Thanks boss and thanks for everything, you gave me a second chance and I'm grateful for that.'

He nodded, we shook hands and just then my car arrived.

'Godspeed.'

So off to London and my first introduction to the world of first-class travel-wow! First class lounge is amazing, free food, booze and movies to watch. I took it easy with the booze, I am working after all. The seat on the plane was massive and despite the funny looks I got from some of the other passengers, (in civvies I usually look like Worzel Gummidge's scruffy cousin) I settled in well.

I thoroughly enjoyed the flight to Chicago, I even stayed awake as I was too excited to sleep. I was still using a metal walking stick that the physio had given me, I had to hand it to the crew when I boarded but they always gave it back to me when I left.

Just as I was deplaning (fancy, I know) a young woman in a business suit came up to me.

'Mr Naismith, will you follow me please?'

Have I been rumbled I thought, was the new identity a bit wobbly? I wondered if there was a problem because a few weeks ago I had entered the USA through Los Angeles and left in a mess with my feet bleeding. I am fairly sure that the DHS did not stamp my passport on the way out, anyway I had a different, suitably worn, passport in my pocket.

You know in an airport there are loads of doors with no signs on and you wonder where they lead to? Well I do, I am a bit curious that way. She led me through one of them, down some stairs and into a small office where there was another woman with an Immigration uniform and a stamp for my passport. She accepted my legal entry into the USA and as I was leaving said very quietly,

'We are all very happy that you are here.'

Ok. All as in who, US Immigration? I don't think so, I strongly suspect she was a friend of Senator Bob, a bit like being a friend of Dorothy but without the excitement and nice clothes.

I wandered about the airport in a bit of a daze, what an amazing place, this is what Brize Norton should look like! Shops, places to eat, bars. Places to buy luggage, why I thought? Do some people turn up for their flight with their clothes in carrier bags and then decide to buy what seemed to me to be some very expensive luggage? I don't know.

Soon enough they called my flight and I was off to Billings, Montana, sounds very romantic but apparently it isn't. I had done some research in the library at the camp on the basis that I might have to

Escape and Evade from a situation that had gone to rat-shit but all I remembered from the maps is that anywhere else is a very long way away from Billings, Montana.

Again I enjoyed the flight although it was a lot shorter than the first one at just under three hours. I deplaned and as I walked into the airport building I wondered who was meeting me and would they be standing there with my name handwritten on a piece of card just like you see on the movies.

I was using my stick and I was hobbling a bit as my hip had started hurting from sitting still on the two flights I had been on. There she was, possibly the most beautiful woman I had ever met, Cassie was waiting for me and as soon as she saw me she burst into tears. Oh dear.

She was wearing jeans and a check shirt and a cowboy hat but she still looked fabulous.

'What have they done to you?'

'It's not as bad as it looks.'

Actually it was, I was not healing as quickly as we had expected, my temporary teeth were still a mess and Dr. J. thought that there might be some residual PTSD effects which were slowing down my body's natural healing processes. She had given me a book to read called, 'The body keeps the score,' great book but the first few chapters frightened the crap out of me, gave me horrendous nightmares and it was currently sitting unread on my bookshelf back at the base.

Cassie put her arms around me but I winced with the pain and she pulled back and started crying even more. Luckily, she was not the only person crying in the airport arrivals hall and so we did not look too much out of place.

'Why did you not tell them what they wanted to know, they would have stopped hurting you?'

'No way,' I said, scoring massive amounts of Brownie points, hoping in the near future that 'Points would mean Pussy.' Yes, still shallow.

'You guys had trusted me; I would die rather than give you up.'

Plus, I thought it was you guys doing the hitting and that you were going to kill me if I talked but I kept that to myself. I was only carrying a small backpack as I planned to buy new stuff over here. I had left most of my good stuff in LA including a very nice mountain bike. Before Colin had told me about my compensation money I had gone to the admin office at the camp to see if I could claim for it but they said no, it was an 'Act of God'. They did laugh a lot when they said it so I suppose I will have to follow my own advice about taking a joke. Fair enough.

We went outside to a massive red Ford F150 pickup, thing is it didn't look out of place, it was not the biggest truck in the car park and it was covered in dust so it looked really authentic. We drove to a big hotel about half-an-hour out of town. Cassie explained that this would be a quarantine stop, that she would have to check me for any kind of communications device (good shout Colin) and we would stay a couple of days in case anyone from either side was trying to follow me.

We had a massive suite with two double beds, a sitting room, small kitchen area, a balcony with amazing views of distant mountains and a jacuzzi in the bathroom, (yes, you know what I am thinking and yes you are correct, soap bubbles are a great lubricant!) and also the warm water would ease my injuries.

I was knackered by this time having for once in my life failed to fall asleep on an aircraft. Cassie switched the jacuzzi on and then asked me to strip. She went over my whole body with what looked like one of the wands that security guards have to check you for weapons. Fortunately, there were no beeps, we had discussed some form of communications tracking implant but we have a lot of respect for these people and that proved to be correct.

She even slipped a rubber glove on and checked to see if I had a spare radio stuck up my arse, I didn't and to be fair it was not as enjoyable as I had once imagined it would be.

I had a long hot soak in the jacuzzi and fell asleep. She had taken all of my clothes and they had been burnt, apparently there is some form of radioactive chemical that you can soak into clothing and then you can track the wearer by satellite. Give me a break.

She had brought me some very nice new clothes including cowboy boots, jeans, check shirts, a stockman's coat whatever that is and Stetson cowboy hat which had cost over three thousand dollars and which we had to get steamed to fit my head at the first opportunity. Colin would have pissed himself laughing and so would everyone I have ever met.

After the bath I crawled into bed and fell asleep, too tired to even think about sex, or was that the PTSD? - scary. The next morning I woke up very early from the jetlag. Madam was sleeping next to me so Madam was woken up by my dick pressing in her back then she was turned over and given a thoroughly good rogering-result!

I meant to check the condom for any blood as this was the first time since the torture that anyone else had been involved in my orgasm but I didn't want Cassie thinking that I had radioactive sperm that could be seen by astronauts. Then I fell asleep again.

We stayed for two days in the hotel, it wasn't unpleasant and helped me get over the jetlag. There were lots of new movies I could order up and the food was great. We spent a fair bit of time talking, apparently by holding out under torture I had proved myself ten times over and there would be no more tests for me. I had a drink in the evenings and was surprised to find that Cassie didn't.

She also didn't do oral, although she was always ready to have normal sex, fine by me. I did notice that she didn't seem to get very aroused during sex, I tried all of the tips I had been given all those years ago by my Naafi manageress mentor but none of them worked.

I did eventually think that because she was so spectacularly beautiful that she had never had to make any effort to attract a man and so the sex was mainly physical for her rather than emotional. Bizarrely, there were a couple of times after we arrived at the ranch that I ended up thinking about Lisa during sex just so I could come with Cassie, weird I know.

Cassie explained that the ranch we were going to was very remote and was the national HQ for TAB. It was just about immune from eavesdropping and it was where they held the high-level meetings of the Re-Founding Fathers. I would be on hand to keep the UK in touch with what was happening so that we could pull our troops out of any hazardous areas well in advance.

The communication system was really simple, I would pick an American vehicle at random from a brochure and send an imaginary evaluation report back to Hereford containing the new information. The report would be coded, they would deliver the one-time code to Colin the day before I sent the update and the UK would be fully briefed. Genius really.

On the third day we set off again in the pickup. I was feeling like a pillock wearing my new cowboy clothes but Cassie liked them and to be fair everyone else was wearing them so I didn't look out of place. The boots weren't worn in yet so I had some very expensive trainers to wear in the meantime.

We drove for several hours until we arrived at the nearest sizeable town to the ranch which was Glasgow. Yes really, Glasgow Montana, there is even a Glasgow Airport which is where I would be collecting and dropping off some of the visitors. Ostensibly the visitors would be coming for hunting and fishing breaks and the ranch minibus was sign written with the adventure company's details.

About an hour later we were driving through fabulous open countryside and my first thought was that I needed to get a big dirt bike and go off exploring all of this amazing area. A long dirt road led us eventually to the biggest surprise of the day, the ranch. Wow! I was expecting something like South Fork what I saw was more like the Addams Family.

The main house was a three-story gothic style monstrosity. Apparently built in the last century by a railroad millionaire who after his death was found to be suffering from the mentally debilitating effects of syphilis. I suppose it was funny really but it did look like you could film horror movies in it. There were number of more conventional agricultural type buildings scattered about at the rear of the house but the initial view as you approached from the road was really a shock.

The guy had also been obsessed with eastern mysticism and religions and named the ranch, 'Nandana,' which is apparently the Sanskrit word for paradise. So 'Paradise Ranch' was the name of the company, calling it that saved having to explain the origins of the name to any visitors.

Whilst it operated as a hunting and fishing retreat you could not book it on Expedia or in fact any other website, visits were strictly by invitation only. Any enquiries to the phone number or web address painted on the van would elicit only the information that the facility was fully booked for the near future.

This made it an ideal place for senior military officers, business leaders and politicians to visit for weekends, any journalistic interest was squashed by TAB supporters in the media companies.

It was a great place to live although we were now in the grip of the Montana winter. Surprisingly, I really enjoyed myself, it was a dry cold not the wet miserable weather we get in England and the countryside was spectacular. Some TAB supporters from the local area came in everyday to maintain the property, clean the house and cook our meals but if we did not have official visitors then Cassie and I were alone at nights.

I had my first introduction to snowmobiles, what a hoot. I started with a standard one but then bought a couple of high-performance ones, Yamaha and Polaris and all of the gear. I would often go off during the week for a full day into the hills and countryside with food, water and a survival pack. Big boys toys really.

Most weekends were busy as a variety of people flew in and out including Senator Bob, who was not a senator and whose name was not Bob, go figure. He turned out to be a very senior CIA officer named David. He was very apologetic when we met up again, they had lost track of me after the first session in California only hearing about my predicament by monitoring the communications coming from Hereford.

They had TAB people on the base at Ramstein which is why they beat us to it. He also told me that the manager in DHS who had authorised my torture had been killed in a very unfortunate incident when his car had caught fire. Serious men indeed, I am all for payback but wow.

This continued throughout the winter apart from one incident that I had to think about. I had driven the minibus down into the nearest town to stock up on my personal supplies of clothing, booze and toiletries. Whilst I was in town I went to the diner for a coffee and some pancakes.

Cassie liked a healthy diet which is why she always looked so spectacular but kale and quinoa were not really enough for a growing lad like myself, although I had lost a little weight, had largely recovered from my injuries and was feeling better than I had ever felt in my life.

I always locked the vehicle when I left it although I think I was the only person in northern Montana who did. When I opened the door I saw a plain envelope on the passenger seat. I opened it and read the message. Crap, what to do?

I drove slowly back to the ranch, went straight in and showed the note to Cassie. It was handwritten on plain paper and it read.

'Sgt Lewis,

We need to set up some comms that TAB cannot access. Please phone this number next time you are getting supplies ***************.

Colin W.'

Cassie said that she would sort it out and that she needed to report this to the TAB network. I should leave it with her, I should not phone the number and I should tell her if there were any more contacts. I agreed with her and said that the work we were doing here was too important to risk.

Silly cow, thinking I would fall for that. Since the first time I had met him at Colchester, Colin had only ever called me Michael. In fact he was the only person who ever did, most people using my nickname or just Mike. The idea that he would suddenly start writing to me as Sgt Lewis was just too hysterical for words. Still it did mean that despite everything that I had been through they did not trust me one hundred percent. Stay alert mate I thought, keep your eye on the prize not the pussy. Although I would try to do both if you get my meaning.

33.

I came awake slowly and looked at the clock, 3.15 in the morning WTF? I could hear a soft chiming that seemed to be sounding all the way through the house, Cassie was sitting up in the bed next to me.

'They are coming,' she said,

'Who?'

'The government, it's the start of the beginning. We need to warn the network. It's time to initiate FFD.'

Shit, FFD was not planned for another couple of months but if the authorities were onto us then she would need to alert everyone. I slipped my clothes on and splashed some water on my face, Cassie was getting dressed and I followed her downstairs.

The chiming was continuing,

'How do you know they are here?'

'The house alarms are ringing; they must be up at the staging area planning their assault.'

The staging area was a big turning area out of view of the house about eight hundred meters away. There were some old fence posts there but nothing else, I suppose that if you were planning to raid the ranch then that would be a good place to gather your troops. Also a bit obvious which is why they had alarm sensors out there.

'What do we need to do?'

''Nothing,' she said, 'The house will do it all.'

'What do you mean?'

'They publish all of their assault tactics on the Internet, the house was designed to protect us even if we are dead. All of the defences are automatic, we can watch from the bunker.'

Bunker? There isn't a bunker, I have been here for months and have never seen any sign of a bunker?

I followed her to a corridor just off the kitchen and she opened a door into what I had thought was a broom cupboard. She then reached through to the back wall, I heard a click and saw the door in the back wall opening. We went through and down some steps, at the bottom was a steel door which opened into a room about the size of a shipping container.

Crazy, I never knew about this one. One side of the room had several tv screens on the wall and when Cassie switched them on we saw 360-degree views of the outside of the house including the staging area, this was full of vehicles and people in combat gear milling about. There were about twenty well-spaced troops making their way across the fields at the front of the house wearing night vision gear.

On the other wall was a desk with a computer and monitor, there was a big Smith and Wesson revolver on the desk, a couple of jerrycans on the floor and a grenade duct-taped to a leg of the table. Cassie sat at the desk and fired up the computer.

'What's happening?'

'This is the last stand; I am going to alert the network so that they can take over the country now. Then we empty the fuel cans and kill ourselves.'

She looked up at me.

'I am really glad you are here; you can shoot me please, then blow the grenade and everything will be destroyed so they cannot get the information. By this evening America will be saved.'

Sorry, hold on just one minute there Mrs. I had not been invited to this party so I might have to Foxtrot. (Military slang - Foxtrot Oscar – leave the area at speed!)

'Let's not rush into this,' I said. 'What's happening with the Feds?'

We looked at the screens and saw that the troops were about one hundred metres from the house. Then the screen went dark.

'The house will fire a very bright flickering light at them. It will blind them temporarily and cause seizures in anyone who is susceptible.'

The screens came back on and I could see the figures staggering about, some of them were lying on the floor and thrashing about. Wow.

'The fenceposts at the turnaround have Claymores in, they should be firing about now,'

And they did, shit. Claymore mines fire a burst of ball bearings and are meant to defend your position from an enemy. The effect on the vehicles and people in the turnaround was catastrophic. They were basically shredded.

'Now they will regroup until dawn so that the lights won't affect them next time they attack.'

And they did, that's the problem with telling everybody what you are going to do, the house had been built to mirror an assault by the Federal Government.

The walls were apparently bulletproof behind the wooden outer skin and were filled with explosive that would detonate eight minutes after any of the external doors were opened. That would give an attacking force just enough time to be all of the way inside the building when it blew. The plan was that when Cassie sent the 'go' signal to the network, key people in the government and military would take over their areas and the whole TAB process would start. They were powerful enough to do this today.

'How do you send the signal then?' I asked, trying to sound enthusiastic.

'Watch this,' she said, 'You are witnessing history.'

She used a retina scanner and a fingerprint reader to fire up the computer, then tapped a few buttons until she got the control screen up. That was when I picked up the big revolver and shot her in the side of the head.

Fuck! that was loud, I had forgotten that we were in a steel box underground, the noise made my ears ring. Cassie was down on the floor and was very dead, I put the pistol in her hand and laid it out as if she had shot herself.

I sat at the computer grabbed a pen and piece of paper and sketched out my code words which I then converted into numbers. I typed the numbers into the search box and ended them with @GCHQ. I thought about what I was doing, thought about some of the improvements that TAB would be making to America, to the lives of ordinary people, poor people lost in what is currently a very corrupt system ruled by big business.

Then I remembered my recruit training all of those years ago. One of the instructors was a big fan of Winston Churchill, he would often talk about him when we were out on field training in the middle of nowhere. I only really remembered one thing he said and that was something about democracy being the worst form of government, except for all the others.

I pressed enter and waited. The machine chuntered away for about a minute. I had been careful with the numbers, all they had was a long string, they would not be able to identify the words I had used I am sure. No? It took them under two minutes, there was a fanfare of noise from the screen and then a glorious technicolour picture. Pugh, Pugh, Barney McGrew, Cuthbert, Dibble and Grubb- The

Trumpton Fire Brigade, OK so they cracked the code, they were GCHQ after all.

The next problem I had was getting out of here in one piece. I opened the lids on the jerrycans, no need to slosh it about, the fumes would do the work. I sprinted up to the kitchen and grabbed some fishing line from a drawer. I had to blow these computers to give GCHQ as much of a head start as possible.

I ran back down into the bunker and tied the line to the pin on the grenade after checking that it would slide out smoothly. I legged it back upstairs trailing the fishing line behind me and went searching in the kitchen, I found a white tea-towel and a broom handle. I know, I know, I am the last person who should be relying on a white flag but needs must etc because the devil was definitely driving now.

I duct-taped the towel to the broom and went to check the front door, there was very little action outside as they had not come in for the second wave yet. I yanked the fishing line and felt it come loose, hoping that there was a decent fuse on the grenade, I opened the door and stuck the flag out. The grenade blew and there was an explosion from the bunker but it wasn't too bad, I think because I had opened the door I had let some of the blast pressure out. The petrol had ignited and I could smell burning.

People were screaming at me from outside, I threw out the flag, put both hands out in front of me and stepped slowly through the door. I had only gone a couple of steps when I was thrown to the ground, searched and handcuffed.

'It's going to blow, the house is going to blow, it's going to blow!'

Fortunately, the guys who had grabbed me were an FBI Hostage Rescue Team, reckoned to be almost the equivalent of the blades. Almost, because the HRT had to operate within the law, the regiment not so much. They were very professional and did not shoot me, I would probably have shot me, but that's just me-lol! The team leader yelled,

'When is it going to blow?'

'Eight minutes from the door opening,'

'Is there anyone alive in the house?'

Sensible question in the circumstances,

'No, no one else,'

'Where is the woman?'

'She shot herself, that's why I could get away.'

Thought I had better plant that story right from the start.

'You have got to get away, the house is a trap, she has blown the computers anyway,'

'OK,'

'Do you have a code word for me sir?'

'Goldstone, goldstone'

That was on the last note Julia had given me and it worked for me now.

He waved his hand and a black assault vehicle showed up, we piled in the back, me still with the handcuffs on and sped down the drive. Everyone pulled back and sure enough just before eight minutes the house blew, fuck me there must have been a shedload of explosives in the place because anyone in or around it would have been incinerated.

They had set up a long way back from the turnaround where there were still CSI vans combing through the wreckage, not a job I would have fancied. They used a fingerprint reader on me to check who I was then took the cuffs off. The team leader shook my hand.

'I don't know what you were doing in the house sergeant but I am sure glad that you were able to warn us about the bomb.'

'I am grateful that you were able to get me out sir, I think both of us will be doing a shitload of paperwork over this.'

He laughed.

I was then taken to meet the boss, the lead agent in charge, a middle-aged black woman sitting in the back of a black Chevy Suburban. She did tell me her name but I was zoning out a bit now. I had been undercover without any kind of training or backup for almost five months and I was knackered. Yes, I had been shagging a spectacularly beautiful woman for all of that time but hey, someone has to do the difficult jobs that no one else wants.

She was asking me questions but kept getting interrupted by people checking on the casualties from last night and wanting orders for what they were going to do next with the ranch.

Then she got a phone call, she kept answering someone as 'Director' and then told the driver to head out back towards town. We set off and she explained,

'They are sending a helicopter for you; they want you back in Washington as soon as possible.'

Washington, the big time, although I did envisage a lot of boring offices, endless questions and not much time off to see the sights. We drove down the road, she was sitting behind the driver and I sat next to her, after about twenty minutes we saw the lights of a chopper over to the right so the driver turned off the road into a field where there was room for the Blackhawk to land on our left.

As usual clouds of dust, loads of noise and it was down, about fifty metres away. The side door opened and two guys wearing full military gear and carrying assault rifles jumped out, I was still zonked at this stage but I was getting a very bad feeling about this.

I was right, they lifted the rifles and started shooting at the Chevy, aiming at the windows. Fuck. I grabbed the pistol from the agents shoulder holster just as her head exploded and rolled out of my door which was fortunately on the side away from the chopper.

All those hours on the indoor range at Hereford finally paid off. I hit the ground with the weapon cocked and ready to go. Squinting under the truck I saw two sets of legs so I shot the nearest guy in his left ankle and his mate in his right ankle. They both went down like someone who had been shot in the ankle at close range. The guy nearest me landed facing towards me so I shot him in the face, the other guy fell backwards and twisted away from me so I shot him right up the arse, bastard.

I rolled to my right so that I was behind the front wheel and the engine. I popped up, rested my hands on the bonnet and sighted on the pilots window. My first shot was high but the next three weren't and I saw the pilot slump forwards in his seat. I ran around the back of the truck and saw that the guy I had shot up the arse was still moving so I shot him in the throat. I was running on automatic now and sprinted towards the chopper to see if there was anyone else inside, there wasn't.

It was still running with the rotors turning so I checked everyone out and they were all dead. Shit. I started to breathe a little easier as I tried to decide what to do next. Have you ever had one of those days when you wished that you had learned how to fly a helicopter? Well I was having one now.

The Chevy was still running as the bad guys had only fired at the windows. I took the rifles from the two assaulters but they did not have grenades or anything that could help me blitz this chopper, I was not leaving it for whoever came looking for me.

You might think it is easy to disable a helicopter, not so. I had seen them in Afghan absolutely shot to shit and still flying, even after a crash landing and losing the undercarriage they can still lift off and fly. Also all of the electrics and hydraulics systems have duplicates and triplicates to help them keep running.

But then I remembered, there were not enough tables in the mess.

34.

Some time ago the regiment had moved to the new site and some numpty in planning had decided that as blades were out on operations for a lot of the time then you did not need enough tables in the mess for all of the residents. This meant that I often had to share a table with other members. Not really a problem as I was still very welcome in the mess. I would concentrate on my meal and the guys would continue their conversations.

I remembered hearing one group discussing the difficulty of disabling helicopters. They had been on a very hush-hush operation in a country which produces a lot of illegal drugs, starts with C ends in an A and is not Canada. The opposition had some Huey helicopters which were proving very difficult to shoot down or damage when they were on the ground.

The collected wisdom was that the best option was to attack the tail rotor. This was the most vulnerable part of the aircraft because if you could stop it working then the chopper turned into a giant food mixer and would shake itself to death trying to turn the fuselage with the rotors.

I picked up one of the assault rifles, gripped it by the barrel and hurled it at the tail rotor, bang on. It smashed into the rotor which then disintegrated and the chopper started spinning, one point they did not tell me was that if you do this then you have to run like F**k because pieces of the chopper will be flying in all directions.

I was hiding behind the Chevy until the bits stopped flying about but at least the Blackhawk was not going anywhere now, except to the scrapyard. The Chevy was still running so I dragged the driver and lead agents bodies out and left them on the ground. I needed a sharp knife and found a big combat knife on one of the gunmen. This model of truck has a GPS unit under the bonnet which I needed to lose. I found it and sliced all of the wires off so no one could track me. But this was an FBI vehicle and I knew that they had their own tracker fitted near the rear axle so I slid under the back end and cut all of the wires on that one as well.

Now it was definitely time for me to bug out. I had a plan in place which I had managed to set up not long after I arrived at the ranch.

I drove the Suburban back towards the ranch heading up a track into the hills about two miles away from the turnaround. The track led up to an area of rugged forest and an old cabin I had found when I first started exploring my surroundings. Cassie had asked me to go and hunt coyotes in the forests as all of the local ranchers hated them attacking their domestic animals and cattle.

I was still having problems with my hip and struggling to ride a motorcycle so I went into town and using the ranch business account I bought myself a big Honda four-wheel-drive quad bike a cracking piece of kit. I bought a hunting rifle with a scope and a 'bear setup,' This was a .357 magnum revolver and a chest holster used so that the pistol is always a few inches from your hand. I loaded the first two chambers with blanks and the last four with some heavy slug ammunition. My hope was that the bear would be scared off by the blanks and if not then it would get four shots in the throat.

I bought all of the camouflage / bright orange hunting gear, there's a contradiction for you, and spare fuel cans. I kept the quad bike and all the kit up at the cabin and would drive up there in the ranch pickup then take the smaller quad bike up the narrow forest tracks which covered the area. I quickly realised that the Canadian border into Saskatchewan was only just over one hundred miles away and could be reached by forest trails. This was my escape route. I kept the quad fully fuelled with supplies of canned food, water and ammo ready to go.

As for the coyotes, I set up in a camo hide at one point with the rifle and watched one coming down in the evening looking for food. I had a clear shot but decided not to shoot, I could recognise a kindred spirit when I saw one. Shoot people yes, animals no.

The cabin had a lean-to shelter at the side and I managed to cram the Chevy into it under cover, it should not be visible from the air. I figured that if I got going quickly then by the time anyone came looking for me I would be far enough away from the incident site to be just another hunter, wearing a bright orange vest, hiding in plain sight.

I had good maps and I had covered a lot of the trails previously so the first couple of hours went ok but as the forest became denser and there were fewer tracks I started struggling, sometimes having to back up and try alternatives when the trees were too close together. After about eight hours of really hard riding I came to some signs announcing the

Canadian border. The path was blocked by a steel gate with a big lock on it. My big rifle beat their big lock, one-nil, and I was through and riding illegally down into Canada.

Another hour and I arrived in a small town just as it was getting dusk. I quickly realised that I blended in perfectly as there were guys in hunting gear all over the place. I needed a phone and saw a diner on the corner of a street. I parked the quad, went in and ordered a coffee, it was a border town so they were happy to take US dollars and went to the phone.

I dialled the long number, didn't need money for this one, two rings then a very welcome voice said, 'Zero'.

'Zero, this is 519, (my callsign) Hotel-X-ray, over,'

Hotel X-ray is the code for a 'hot extraction,' basically I was in the shit and needed rescuing.

'Wait one,'

They wanted me to wait one minute, it was a bit longer than that. I knew that they would have my location from the phone so I guessed that they would need time to make a plan.

I waited about five minutes then,

'519 this is Sierra 2, are you mobile over?'

'Yes, over,'

'Wait 30 minutes at your location then travel north, recognition is two long one short received over?'

'Two long, one short, received over.'

He was the boss I was not going to end the call.

'Sierra 2 outstanding, out.'

The last bit wasn't strictly procedure but it seemed like I had done something right for once. So wait thirty minutes in a diner, how could I pass the time? Bacon, eggs, pancakes and hash browns all slathered in maple syrup, now that was outstanding.

Thirty minutes passed quickly; I left the waitress a good tip as I did not think I would be using US dollars again anytime soon. I fired up the quad and headed north as instructed. I had been riding for about an hour and was just thinking of a comfort break and a refuelling stop when I saw it coming in low and fast in front of me, yes my favourite helicopter, the Chinook. I started flashing my headlight, two long one short and received an answering flash from the aircraft's lights.

The big chopper turned away from me and landed in a field of crops at the side of the road, I headed for it and the tail ramp came down.

The loadie was waving me in as I got there so I rode straight up the ramp into the load space. I switched the engine off and jammed the brakes on until he got a big blue ratchet strap around the bars and locked it down, I climbed off and he put another strap around the rear rack.

The chopper had taken off by this time and we were heading to what I hoped was safety. The loadie handed me a headset but this time I was wired into the aircrafts communications, a very welcome voice said,

'Michael, how are you?'

'Fine sir, thank you,'

'Great job at the ranch, Julia got everything. Outstanding, see you when you get back,'

'Roger that sir.'

The loadie then came on the net and asked me to clear my weapons. This would be for the safety of the aircraft. I emptied the revolver and put the rounds in my pocket, showed him the empty weapon and he nodded. I went to the front of the quad; the hunting rifle was in a locked frame with no magazine on. I took the bolt out and left it on the seat.

The loadie gave me some water which I took and a lunch box which I didn't. We flew for about an hour and then landed on a dark airbase and taxied straight into a hangar. There was a female Canadian Air Force sergeant waiting for me and she took me to a table where a flight suit and helmet had been set out. Apparently we were at Canadian Forces Base, Moose Jaw which had been the nearest place to my extraction point.

This was a training base using two-seater jets.

'Can you get changed please sir we need to get going?'

Ok chuck, let's get going and we did in a flight of six aircraft doing one of their usual training routines flying across Canada until we taxied into a hangar at CFB Goose Bay several hour later. At one point the pilot let me fly it for a couple of minutes, great experience but I could not find the handbrake so I thanked him very much and decided to stick to wheels and tracks.

I climbed out of the trainer and I looked round the hangar and then I saw my next lift, fuck me, an RAF jet fighter. Not sure which one but it looked like it was doing a thousand miles an hour just sitting on the concrete. Wow!

I kept the flight suit on and walked over to the aircraft. A guy I assumed was the pilot came up to me, he looked to be about twelve and had a really intense manner about him. I suppose you needed to be a bit intense to fly fast jets. He told me his name but I just thought of him as Biggles and started zoning out again I was really tired.

'I said, who are you and why am I flying you to the UK?'

Crap, I must have missed the first part of the question.

'I cannot tell you that sir, but if the US military realise that I am in this plane then they will blow us out of the sky.'

'This is unacceptable,' he said, 'I will get these orders changed, I am not risking my aircraft for some special forces nonsense.'

He wandered off and another woman sergeant started briefing me on life in the fast jet cockpit. She gave me a bottle of water, a bag to be sick in and a tube bladder type device to piss in. Fair enough.

Biggles came back after a couple of minutes and said,

'Right then let's get going,'

Obviously, he had received the good news from someone higher up in the food chain.

I climbed up a ladder and the woman helped me in. Shit, it was even more cramped than the Canadian trainer jets. I thought armoured vehicles were tight inside but this was ridiculous. She belted me in and basically told me not to touch anything. OK. She showed me the handle for the ejector seat and made sure I was ready when she took the safety pins out of the mechanism.

'The pilot will shout eject, eject, eject, you pull the lever and you will be out, the aircraft will not let you both eject at the same time so there may be a couple of seconds delay.'

Now I was really scared, no really, the thought of being blasted into the sky from a crashing fighter jet was so far outside my experience I was getting the shakes. Fortunately, I could not move very much so I just practised some of Dr. J.'s breathing exercises and tried to stay calm.

Biggles climbed in and seemed to be in a huff, he didn't say much just told me not to touch anything, especially the ejector handle. Well he was ok there I was not going to touch fuck all until we were home and dry.

We rolled out onto the tarmac and started to taxi, he was talking to the tower but it did not make much sense to me, I could not relax just yet. Then we reached the runway and he spooled the engines up with the brakes on and then we took off. Hell this thing could accelerate, then we were flying, we turned away from the airfield and started climbing, this went on for ages then I fell asleep. To be fair I had been up since 3.15 fighting for my life so I reckon I was entitled to a nap.

He was shouting at me over the intercom,

'Sir, sir, are you awake?'

Oh crap, do I have to eject? No he wasn't saying that and the roof was still on so I think we were ok.

'What, yes I'm awake.'

'Look outside,'

I did, there must have been a dozen of them, RAF jet fighters just like this one surrounding us really close, bit like the Red Arrows do, hopefully that would put the Yanks off if they still wanted to whack me. A few minutes later we were landing, in the dark on a big base somewhere which I hoped was the UK.

'Welcome to Brize,' he said.

Thank you, thank you, thank you. I was back where I had left from last March when I went to Batus. Brize Norton, England now I could relax. Never mind the glitz and glamour of Chicago airport this was home for me. We taxied into a hangar out of sight of any pesky satellites. Another RAF woman helped me get out of the cockpit after she had locked the ejector seat. I started taking the flight suit off when Colin appeared and shook my hand. He seemed happy.

Biggles climbed out and just looked at me then walked away in a huff, well I thought, FUCK HIM IF HE CAN'T TAKE A JOKE! Yes, I was losing it again. Colin was chuntering about stuff and then we went and sat in a little crew room drinking decent coffee and he brought me up to speed. GCHQ had cracked the TAB computer network and authorities on both sides of the Atlantic were busy wrapping up the membership. There had been two TAB people in the regiment, one had met with an unfortunate training accident and one was currently answering questions in a dusty basement room somewhere. I think given the choice I would have chosen the accident.

Colin pointed me towards a laundry van parked in the corner of the hangar.

'This is your ride; you are off to a safe house for debriefing. I may not see you again because you are going to be off the grid now but thank you for everything.'

'It's been a hoot Major, an absolute blast. Cheers'

What else could I say, he got me out of one shit situation and ended up dropping me into two other ones. I wouldn't have changed it though, apart from getting my arse kicked.

We waited until nightfall and then I left the hangar in the back of the laundry van. We drove for ages and then stopped inside another smaller garage. A middle-aged woman was waiting for me and said,

'Good evening sir welcome to Saltbox Farm, we are in Norfolk about thirty miles from Norwich. I am Mrs McIntyre the house manager. I will show you to your room. We just have a couple of house rules please. Stay indoors, we have a gym and a swimming pool and we do not want you being seen by any satellites.

Please do not exchange any personal information with any of the other guests, mealtimes are very flexible, we have a free bar but please drink responsibly. If you do need any medical attention there is a phone in your room and there is an operator on duty 24 hours. If there is anything we can do please just ask. Finally, if you do hear gunfire at any time please stay in your room, we have very effective security measures and you will come to no harm.'

'Thank you very much.'

I slept very well and was pleasantly surprised to see Dr. J. the following morning. We had sessions for the first three days and then she said that there was nothing more that she could do for me. So either I was cured or completely bonkers or more probably both at the same time - lol.

35.

It was a couple of months later that I landed in New Zealand. The debriefing on the Norfolk farm had taken a few weeks longer than expected as I had to repeat my account of the past few months to a range of untitled and unacknowledged spooks, often having American accents. We had also laboured long and hard over the decisions about my new identity. We decided that I would be Australian, staying as far away from North America and most of Europe as possible seemed to make the most sense.

Plenty of places to disappear in that vast continent with the favourite places to settle being Melbourne in the east or Freemantle in the west, both equally good choices I thought. I had taken daily lessons from a professional accent coach and now spoke most of the time like an Australian citizen who had lived in the UK for an extended period of time. I relapsed and got a bit 'northern' when I was drunk but that was just another reason to stay reasonably sober and not let my guard down.

Apparently, the list of people from TAB wishing to do me harm was growing longer by the day. Yes, the FBI, DHS and sundry other three letter agencies had rounded up the ringleaders and identified most of the membership but the American court process, the process that ironically TAB wished to abolish, was grinding very slowly and many of the members were out on bail and free to seek out yours truly for some payback.

Speaking of payback, the US government had come through with a ten million-dollar pay-out for my efforts leaving me with a cool four million for myself. That amount added to my previous pay-out meant that I was very wealthy indeed so a laid-back life in the Australian sun beckoned. It also meant that Ian Naismith could at last have a funeral service and his name on the clock memorial at Hereford. I always raised the first glass to him every time I had a drink. Godspeed mate.

So, what am I doing in Auckland then you ask? Looking for Lisa as always, before I make any decisions about my future I really need to know how things stand with her. I had been here for two weeks and had managed to find a female run private detective agency that was willing to help me out (for a fee).

So, 1000 NZ dollars lighter I had now discovered that Lisa was still single, but also more importantly that she is not currently in a relationship.

The PI had taken some convincing that I was not some kind of sex mad stalker, but I had agreed with her that if she discovered that Lisa was with someone then I would simply fade away back to Australia and leave her in peace.

The report I read was very clear that Lisa was not currently in a relationship, the PI even having managed to speak with her in a supermarket on the pretence of carrying out a survey on romance.

I had parked the Holden rental car a few doors up the hill from Lisa's bungalow it was 3.45pm and she was due home at 4. There was a garden bench on the front path next to her parking space, I took a deep breath and got out of the car with the bunch of red roses and bottle of champagne in my hands. I also had a packet of condoms in my pocket, thinking positive!

Sitting on the bench I was surprised how nervous I was. I had last seen her a couple of years ago and whilst I felt pretty much the same as I did then, a lot of people had died in the meantime.

Sure enough, just before 4 and her small blue Ford pulled into the parking space. She looked amazing, her hair was shorter and lighter, and I could see her sparkly blue eyes even through the car windscreen. Fantastic. I smiled, left the bottle on the bench and lifted my hand to wave, that was when I heard the clunk of the car going into reverse. She backed slowly out onto the street then turned to look at me. To be fair she looked serious but not hostile or angry. I took that as a positive, then she drove off.

Well, I had mentally rehearsed a number of scenarios for this meeting ranging from frenzied sex right there in the front garden, to a joyous reunion followed by frenzied sex in her bedroom and even a tearful, slightly angry conversation followed by frenzied sex anywhere. Out of luck so far.

Why had she driven off, what was happening? After thinking about it for a few minutes I came up with an answer. I knew that Lisa was not in a relationship, so it was likely that she was wearing comfortable, possibly well washed and faded underwear that she did not want me to see, prior to our frenzied sexual reunion. She must even now be driving to the New Zealand version of Victoria's Secret in order to buy something silky or satiny with lace and straps that would make the overture to our congress even more pleasurable.

In that case I was happy to wait. That was when the cops showed up-shit! Two young officers parked their car by the kerb and walked over towards me. They introduced themselves as senior constable blah de blah and his mate. You can tell that by this stage I was not listening.

I explained that I had known Lisa some time ago and that I had simply called around to see if we could re-kindle the romance. They took my passport and checked it with their control, that was no problem because it was a genuine Australian passport. They asked to search me for weapons, and I emptied my pockets showing them not only the condoms but also the engagement ring I had brought, living in hope eh!

'So, let's just get this straight,' the older one said,

'You brought her flowers, champagne and an engagement ring, and she called the cops on you?'

'Yes,' I said smiling, 'she can be a bit feisty.'

'Well mate' the cop said, 'she does not want to see you, so I think you need to disappear,'

'No problem, I just came to see how things were between us and now I know, I'm off to Australia on the next flight. I'm certainly not some kind of creepy stalker.'

'Fair enough' he said,

'Listen do you guys want some champagne and flowers they are no good to me now' they laughed and said,

'Yes, OK mate.'

It was three months later. I was living in a small bungalow overlooking a beautiful surfing beach in northern Tasmania. I had rented the bungalow for six months so that I could get used to living alone as a civilian. I have told the locals that I was writing a book and that hopefully explained why I wasn't going to all of the social events in the town. I did visit the farmers market every week for veggies and bought fish and shellfish from the local fishermen; I have never had the chance to cook for myself, so I was really enjoying learning.

I started with Gordon Ramsey's book to pick up the basic techniques but then found Nigel Slater's book which introduced a new philosophy to me of cooking a meal from whatever ingredients you had to hand. I have to say there were several occasions when I threw my creations in the bin and had a ride down to the local pizza joint.

I heard the soft chime of the movement detectors, which were disguised as garden lights, on the path up to the bungalow. I glanced through the window and saw Lisa herself, wearing a flowery summer dress walking up the path to the door.

I opened the door and we stood there looking at each other, I stepped out onto the path and kissed her. I pulled her into the house and closed the door behind her. I leaned her back against the door, kissed her for several minutes and then slowly unzipped her dress. It fell to the floor and I left it there. I didn't want a long tearful reunion but I did want a shag. Fuck first, talk later. (that would look good on a T shirt!)

She was wearing pink frilly bra and knickers and she felt really good. She had put a couple of pounds on, but they were good pounds. The guys will know what I mean, her breasts were a little fuller and she's got a little more weight on her hips and her arse which felt amazing. Even more of a good thing. I turned her around and put her hands up on the door as if I was doing a police search, using two hands I undid her bra and dropped it on the floor, I have never been able to undo a bra one handed, I ran my hands down her sides sliding her knickers off on the way. My shorts and T shirt hit the floor and I stepped in close behind her moving my hands up to her naked breasts.

I started pressing my cock against the small of her back. Her nipples were really hard at this point, so it seems pretty likely that she was getting turned on.

I moved my legs between hers pushing them apart, stood with my cock against her bum and kissed her neck. She was gently pushing her bum back at me. Wow.

'Can I fuck you now?' I asked,

Yes, I know it sounds crude, but it felt appropriate, she had come and found me after all.

'Not up my bum, I need to be drunk for that,'

Well, who is being crude now I thought, dangerously close to coming all over her back?

I turned her around to face me and kissed her on the lips, I put my tongue in her mouth and it was just as great as it had been at Hereford. Trying desperately not to come on her stomach I led her through to the bedroom which was just inside the front door. I sat her on the bed and put her hands on my hips which meant that she was just the right height to take my cock in her mouth, she looked up at me teasingly, then very slowly reached out her tongue and licked me.

I pulled away before I gave her a sample of my own organic face cream and took a condom from the bedside table. I handed it to her, and she opened it with her teeth and very slowly put it on me. Always a pleasure.

I pushed her back onto the bed and slipped right into her pussy, there wasn't even the usual resistance at the start, she must have been so aroused, a few strokes and I was done. Wow. A total quickie, but you can't really blame me, the last time I had seen her she had called the cops on me and here she was in my bed sharing a condom. Women. Can't live with them, can't shoot them, unless of course you're in the SAS when apparently you are supposed to shoot them first!

She wriggled away from my attempts at caressing her clitoris and I remembered from our time in Hereford that she sometimes wasn't ready to orgasm just because we were having sex. I had become used to that and didn't take it personally. I had reached my orgasm and that was personal enough for me.

There was a bath towel on the end of the bed in anticipation of my receiving visitors, not my choice but I had a really chirpy, older Greek woman cleaner from the village who came in once a week and she had insisted on being prepared. Good thing really. I reached down for the towel and spread it over her body. I knew that no matter how wild she was during sex as soon as we were finished she became very modest and liked to be covered up.

'Can I get you a drink?'

'White wine please, I'm not driving,'

'Chardonnay or sauvignon?'

'Wow, I'm impressed, have you had a lot of wine drinking visitors lately?'

Typical. She fucks my brains out then gets nosey.

'That's a secret,'

I went back to the hallway collected my shorts, then off to the kitchen where I took two bottles of Stella from the fridge and went back into the bedroom.

I handed one to her,

'My version of white wine madam,'

She laughed, 'I should have guessed.'

'Anyway, Lisa Geraldine Phelan, you have some explaining to do, how did you find me?'

My location was supposed to be as secret as a very secret thing that nobody talks about.

'I went to London and saw Colin Warner, he is working for one of those private military outfits now, he is making an absolute fortune. Once I convinced him I was genuine he had to physically go into Hereford to get your address. I think that he felt he owed me a favour.'

Good old Colin I thought, he might have let me know she was coming though, I could have been playing house with one of the surf bunnies from the village.

'I swore him to secrecy, I wanted to surprise you,'

So much for shooting the women first.

'So then, why did you come to find me, you sent the cops after me last time I saw you?'

She took a deep breath,

'Sorry about that, I was so surprised when I saw you in Auckland. I was scared, I had lost you once after the siege, then again when I left Hereford. I thought you were just there on holiday and I would have to lose you again, I couldn't bear that.'

'OK but what changed your mind?'

'I met one of the cops in the local supermarket, he was there with his wife and daughter. He said that you had retired now and that you had brought me a ring,'

Very softly she said,

'Have you still got the ring?'

I took the little jeweller's box out of the bedside table; I had kept it with the condoms as a souvenir.

I put it on the bed and she just looked at it,

'Open it,'

I did.

'Well?' she said. Looking at me.

OK I'm going to have to work for this, I took a deep breath.

'Lisa Geraldine Phelan, will you marry me?'

'No,' she said, shaking her head.

'No, why did you ask about the ring then,'

'I can't marry you Michael, I can't marry anyone, not after what happened with Max, but I will be your fiancée and wear your ring and share your bed and your life if you will have me.'

I leaned forward and kissed her, she kissed me back and she seemed happy enough, difficult to tell with women.

So, no wedding then, wonder if I can talk her into a wedding night celebration though with one of those white frilly basques, stockings and suspenders that you see in the magazines? (the magazines I read anyway-lol)

'There's just one condition,'

Here we go I thought, this would be a long list of what she won't do in bed. Obviously, I've not been married before but a common complaint from the married blokes I worked with has always been that the sex loving girlfriend they knew, who sucked cock like a demented Hoover, turns into a prudish spinster as soon as they have a ring on their finger. Hence lots of marital break ups when the servicing arrangements break down. Philosophical, I know.

'I want you to put the ring on my finger and I want you to promise me that if you get bored with me, or if you don't want me anymore or if you want to see someone else then you will tell me. I could not bear being betrayed again as I was with Max, I promise I won't make a fuss, I will just go back to Auckland. I need you to put the ring on my finger and if you want me to leave then you just take the ring off my finger and I will go.'

Wow, how long has she been rehearsing that speech? Still I couldn't blame her, Max playing dead and then turning up with another woman and a baby,

I can't imagine what that had done to her. And didn't she just mention anal being a possibility when she was drunk?

I took her hand and slipped the ring onto her finger, it was a bit tight, but we could get it fixed.

'I promise that I will tell you if I want a change and I will be very open and honest with you so there are no surprises. (they only have women's magazines to read in the local Chinese takeaway so I was very familiar with the language of relationships,) but I have a condition as well, I still have a gun and if you are unfaithful to me then I will shoot you in the head, as promised.'

'Ok I agree,' she said laughing.

She thinks I'm joking.

Printed in Great Britain
by Amazon